THE MDSO CHRONICLES THE CROWN JEWELS CAPER

FAB FIVE TAKES ON E.V.I.L

MYRRA OJASVI SHARMA

To my Aita, late Smt. Bimala Phukan, who taught me the importance of believing in fairytales and dreams.

Contents

Foreword

What struck me when I first spoke to Myrra a couple of years ago, was her contagious enthusiasm and high imagination. Not only was she a young girl bursting with stories, she also was curious about the entire writing process. She had a spark in her eyes as she shared her kernel of an idea – about a group of intrepid girls and their adventures.

As I spoke to her about the craft and nuances of writing, she showed a keen interest in how to structure the book and to develop her characters. The discussions were insightful and interesting as we explored the world of writing.

Myrra approached these discussions and worked on her writing with discipline and dedication. This book is a testament to her imagination and hard work. For my part, I will take away her open, curious and enthusiastic attitude – not just towards her writing but life in general. It has been a joy to witness the blossoming of a young writer and I am proud to have been a part of her journey.

Harini Srinivasan
https://harinisrinivasan.com/

Acknowledgements

My sincere thanks and gratitude to my parents for their constant belief and encouragement.

To my sister for unfailingly believing I'm her hero! My extended family for their encouragement. To Ms Harini Srinivasan for her expert guidance and advice. To my teachers at Sunset Elementary and Mendenhall for their words of wisdom and encouragement.

ONE

THE DARSONS

Thump! There was a loud noise from inside the Darson house. Melanie and her mother had planned to start packing at precisely (watch-check) 12 o 'o'clock noon for their much-awaited journey to London. Melanie was particularly thrilled since she had never been there before.

Melanie had just graduated seventh grade, and seventh grade had been the most exciting and friendliest year for Melanie. She had learned so many things and done a lot of homework. Her favorite subjects had to be science or math; she had always been interested in those two subjects since she was a little child. Rumor has it that by the time she was five, she recited the multiplication tables until twenty. Never mind! I am not so sure about the last bit of humblebrag there, but she was intelligent and kind-hearted, even though she was a little blunt.

The middle school in River High was among the better schools in the county and full of students who were motivated to do well. They had a good sports tradition as well as a strong community of parents who volunteered with the school. Raising a family in River High was a slice of suburban living paradise that the Darsons were very glad to have.

School was over, and summer break was now in! She had much more time on her hands for missions and Mother Daughter Secret Organization's work. For now though, relaxed and merry, sleep came easily to her. In fact, she had been sleeping and had the most wonderful dream about doing Mother Daughter Secret Organization work and meeting all her friends. Doing exciting missions, drawing out her favorite gadgets, she was ecstatic until... "Melanie, Melanie, I HAVE BEEN TRYING TO WAKE YOU UP FOR ALMOST AN HOUR. YOU KNOW, say yay for pancakes, yay for packing," said Miss Daisy, Melanie's super Mom.

Melanie's Mom quickly realized that she had made a mistake, waking Melanie up, screaming excitedly. The thought of making hot pancakes with thick blueberry jam and cold cream had made her think that Melanie would be as excited as she was. However, even Miss Daisy had to agree her timing was seriously off.

The truth is, Miss Daisy was just excited to make some pancakes with Melanie. But I think that you probably can tell by now Melanie definitely did not share the excitement.

"Mom, please let me sleep for next year, please," said Melanie, with her pleas intentionally prolonged. Still in bed with her eyes closed, Melanie was a tad bit disappointed because she was having a peaceful and happy dream, but her mother had ruined Melanie's beautiful dream by waking her up. Sensing her daughter's bad mood, Miss Daisy realized she had to do some damage control.

"Ok, fine, I admit it, I am the best Mom EVER, am I right, packing, packing packing?" she said, nudging Melanie continuously. "Right? Am I right, huh, huh?" continued Miss Daisy, persistent about her child partaking in the happiness around pancakes. I mean, who wouldn't be excited about pancakes?

"Ok, fine, fine, I will help you make some pancakes," said Melanie grudgingly, "On one condition you will let me sleep for thirty more minutes after I help you make and then eat the pancakes; do you promise?"

"Mom, promise?" asked Melanie.

Miss Daisy seemed lost in thought, which seldom happened.

"Mother, Mom, Mommy, are you there?" asked Melanie looking at her mother wondering what she was thinking about.

"Oh...sorry, Melanie, I was just thinking about LAUNDRY, yes! To do the laundry exactly, the dishes, the cleaning, and the gardening, the list could go on and on, so I was just thinking about that. You could help sometime, you know, instead of sleeping on your butt the whole day. Aaaand, we need to pack sweetie," said Miss Daisy realizing that her daughter did not quite believe what she had just said.

"Are you fine, Mother?" said Melanie suspiciously.

"Oh, yes I am, positively fine," said Miss Daisy, nervously, biting her nails, knowing that deep down, she was definitely, positively *not* fine.

Miss Daisy had been keeping this secret for a while now, and she was tired of keeping up with her web of secrets and deception with her near and dear ones.

"*Ok, I believe you*, Mother," said Melanie, knowing instinctively, that something was bothering her Mom.

After a long awkward silence, Miss Daisy said, "Ok fine, Let's go make some pancakes, With blueberries and cold cream and banana and chocolate."

"Yes, let's go, I guess; wait, what did you say?" Melanie said.

"Let's go eat some pancakes with blueberries, cold cream, bananas, and chocolate?" repeated Miss Daisy slowly.

"No, Mom, please no banana and cold cream, both are gross. You ought to know by now how much I hate both," yelled Melanie.

Both Mom and daughter stood in silence for a second, Melanie realizing that she had made a mistake by disrespecting her mother.

"Excuse me, young lady, do not raise your voice at me like that, do you understand?" said Miss Daisy sternly, making sure that Melanie got the point loud and clear.

"Geez, sorry, Mom," said Melanie under her breath, murmuring quietly, knowing what was going to happen next.

Her Mom would proclaim, "Whatever you have to say, young lady, say it out loud, muttering is not going to get you anywhere."

"I'm sorry, Mom," Melanie said as they both started to walk.

They both headed downstairs while Melanie ran her fingers along the rail, pondering over what had just happened, and she realized that her Mom had been acting weird the past few months. Miss Daisy acted like she was always hiding something. She always had something she had to get off her chest...but she just could not. Whenever Melanie asked about it, the answer would, predictably, always be the same. It did not matter where, when, or how Melanie brought it up; Miss Daisy just would not say it. Melanie had been wondering if it was all a hoax to distract her from a surprise at first. But then she realized that her Mom had been battling something, something different.

They walked down the long staircase leading to the living room. The Darson house always had a cinnamon smell to it, probably because both Miss Daisy and Melanie loved baking cinnamon rolls and cookies. *A cinnamon stick holds a lot of secrets in its rolls*, thought Melanie as she took in the sights and smells of this wonderful morning. The freshly mowed lawn and the birds chirping about in the garden made her feel more energetic and cheerful already. She could feel this was going to be a wonderful day.

Melanie had lived in this house her whole life. Her parents never had the urge to move and start fresh. They loved their life as is... at least Melanie knew that she did. Melanie's school life was not perfect... to be honest, is anyone's?

Melanie had always been the weird girl at school, she wouldn't get bullied for it though. But for some reason she had felt left out since kindergarten. She did not mind it half of the time, though. She just went on in school with her best friend, Hailey. Hailey was always there for Melanie; like when Melanie and Hailey had their first girls' scope out mission together.

The thought of Hailey brought a smile to her face, and she looked at the pile of unfolded laundry with a distinct lack of enthusiasm.

Pancakes can wait for a tad bit, she thought as she decided she would get started on packing for London. "Mom, I'm going to need about 30 minutes to get through this pile. I'll help after."

TWO

ARE MDSO BFFS LIKE ...FOREVER?

Melanie and Hailey had their first mission together in Paris. They were so excited when the mysterious golden envelope had arrived at their homes.

They had called each other and said, "OH MY GOD! Did you hear we are going on our first mission together?" said Hailey. "Don't you worry, I have gotten everything planned. I have all of our clothing planned out in perfect combinations with matching bracelets and charms. I also have all of our video games and books planned out for every day. Do you think I am missing something?" said Hailey as she ran out of breath.

Melanie rolled her eyes and thought, *typical Hailey, wait, how does she even have my clothes?*" Melanie said aloud, "Hailey, what's the point of getting so excited and overworked for a one-week trip?"

"Because it's PARIS, I am so excited. What did you get assigned as? I got assigned as an assistant to the leader. Sam said that it was based on our test scores and graduation scores."

"Hold on, lemme go ask my Mommy what I got assigned as." Hailey waited for her answer patiently. "Mom said that I got assigned as the group leader. I expect that ought to be exciting", said Melanie, wondering if her best friend was on the same mission assignment as her. Hailey was desperately hoping that the two best friends could go on the same mission. It's almost as if she did not want to jinx it by asking aloud.

The red telephone was shining in the spotlight of the fairly lit room, the table fan was whirring silently just beside Melanie, her hair falling gracefully down onto the telephone while she quietly waited for Hailey to respond. "Hey, Hailey, are you still there?"

"Ya, I am still here; just a random question: which mission are you assigned to?" Hailey asked.

"Oh, I got assigned to the Eiffel Tower problem in Paris. What about you, Hailey?" The phone went silent for a few seconds.

"Really, I got the same mission as you, isn't this so exciting? OMG, I was so worried as I just realized that we could have been on different missions. This is our first mission together, I know you can already tell but I am so excited," screeched Hailey, obviously ecstatic.

"Yes, you did, Hailey, stop screaming," 'said Melanie, secretly happy that she and Hailey would share fun and new adventures. Sometimes, Hailey's energy was too much for Melanie, especially during moments like these when she got so excited.

Hailey had a loud, outgoing personality that bordered on being obnoxious, well, to some people anyway, but not to Melanie. On the other hand, Melanie was quiet, introverted, and very polite. Say what you will, but together, they fit perfectly.

"So, what are you planning to bring on the mission, Melanie?" asked Hailey breathlessly, not being able to contain her excitement.

"I'm not really that sure about that. Hailey, my Mom said something about bringing the gadgets that we had been training with this past year. I'm actually really excited about that. She also said that we had to bring essentials like clothes and our toothbrushes, blankets, pillows, our kits, and most importantly, our phones, lol," said Melanie. "What did your aunt say?" Melanie asked inquiringly.

"My aunt said the same thing." "Ok, fine anyway, what do you plan to bring for the gadgets?" said Hailey.

"I plan to bring multi-bracelets, face-ades, palm-phlets, super glasses, and most importantly... Super Shoes," responded Melanie, happy that Hailey had asked that question because that was Melanie's favorite part about the whole mission. It was not as if she did not like every other part, which was not very surprising because her Mom was a senior executive of Mother Daughter Secret Organization, which meant that Melanie had a lot of responsibilities, including setting an example for every team that she was a part of.

"Wait a second, I forgot what the Super Shoes did, could you remind me?" asked Hailey out of curiosity. Even though she had learned it in training, she was a little forgetful you could say. Not to make excuses but she was so excited at the idea of being in training that sometimes she forgot to actually pay attention to the training class.

"I am happy you asked. So the Super Shoes can freeze water into ice, and can increase your running speed by ten times, make you jump over obstacles, and of course, my personal favorite, is the invisibility booster!" said Melanie explained breathlessly and quickly tried to fit in everything that the Super Shoes did, in one sentence. *She almost forgot to mention that the Super Shoes could turn into a jetpack hoverboard or even a flying hoverboard!*

"Oh, really it can do all of that? THAT IS UNBELIEVABLE, " said Hailey, in awe. "I wonder though why would I need such advanced gadgets, my friend said that she had not had all of these gadgets in her mission training, isn't that weird Melanie?"

"Hailey...wait, did you talk to somebody about our mission already or our training?"

"Maybe?" Hailey said.

"Are you absolutely out of your mind? Our mission coaches said that this was a top-secret mission about which we could say nothing to anybody other than our parents and other trainees," said Melanie in response to Hailey's comment that was very alarming.

"Well... she is a trainee, in a roundabout sort of way," said Hailey.

"Not in our mission, she's not; we could get in serious trouble for this, you know, Hailey," said Melanie worriedly. "What exactly did you tell her?"

"Well...not that much really, just everyone that was in MDSO, the description for every gadget, and the exact coordinates of where the MDSO headquarters were," said Hailey.

"What!" Melanie exclaimed.

"Don't worry, I was just joking," Hailey laughed, Hailey very occasionally did this to Melanie, she said something really serious and revealed that she was just kidding. This was something that Melanie did not appreciate at all.

"Oh my God. Hailey, you have to stop doing that. I was creating scenarios in my head of what they were going to do to you once the mission leaders found out. You are completely crazy. But anyways let's get back to the Super shoes. They are much more interesting than your hopeless pranks" said Melanie angrily.

"It is one of the most advanced pieces of technology in all of MDSO - the inventors spent years trying to formulate this. They had to test it about 290,989,090 times" said Melanie, exaggerating how many times the inventors tested it. In reality, they had only tested the Super Shoes 1802 times, but the larger number of test runs made the Super Shoes sound even more perfect and credible.

"That must have been so tedious, testing the same thing over and over again almost 300 million times," said Hailey, pretty sure Melanie was exaggerating.

"Ok fine, fine, I was lying about how many times they tested the shoes, they only tested it about 1800 times... Sorry."

"You think that I am that stupid to believe that humans could do so many tests?! If they had to do these many tests then the inventors team would have given up on Super Shoes entirely, I think," replied Hailey.

"I mean, umm, fine. I would give up on an invention if it took that many tries, but maybe not... Who knows?" "Yeah, I think I would give up as well if I had to try it a million times, not even a million times, three hundred times, *hahaha*", said Melanie, trying to lighten up the topic.

"HAHA, so funny, Melanie. You definitely did not say that, as I said earlier." "Copycat,'" muttered Hailey sarcastically, under her breath.

"You are such a show-off and a copycat... All you do IS BE ANNOYING. Ugh, I am telling my aunt to take me out of this program."

Hailey had somehow gotten the impression that Melanie was purposely being rude, but all that Melanie had been doing was agreeing with her.

"But-"

"I don't care anymore, " interrupted Hailey.

"I was just trying to be funny and lighten -" Melanie tried again, hoping to salvage the conversation.

"We are not friends anymore," said Hailey, frustrated at Melanie.

"But I did not do anything wrong..." said Melanie angrily, even more bewildered than usual.

"Ok fine... I guess I can let this time pass, AGAIN." said Hailey, slowly understanding that Melanie had just been agreeing with her the whole time."

"WHAT DO YOU MEAN AGAIN, YOU ARE SO OVER-DRAMATIC HAILEY"

Hailey ignored her, knowing that she was right, but was too proud to admit her mistakes.

What a waste this whole argument had been. They were used to doing this. Melanie and Hailey, even though best friends, had frequent fights like this.

"Anyway, let's just plan the mission together." "OK, fine," replied Hailey.

Hailey and Mel both stewed over the last five minutes of their conversation in silence as they both realized simultaneously what a futile argument they just had.

"Ok, let's take a deep breath," Melanie said.

"I am so excited to put all of our learning to use on the trip. We can show all of the older girls how cool we are. Maybe we are even cooler than them," said Hailey enthusiastically.

"I think that is kind of - not the point of the trip... I think that this trip IS TO PROVE what we learned the past year not to the older girls but our coaches and teachers and make them proud, like how to pitch a tent and... stuff," said Melanie in response to what Hailey had thought was a hilarious remark.

"Yeah... I was definitely joking, Melanie," said Hailey.

"Are you sure about that?" Melanie said slowly, not completely convinced about Hailey's response.

"Yes, Melanie I am very sure," said Hailey in astonishment, worried that Melanie was suspicious about her already.

This conversation was certainly not going the way both of them had anticipated. The excitement about going on a mission together was slowly getting colored with a little trepidation and worry.

"Hey, listen, can we pick this up later? My Mom is calling me," Melanie said.

"Umm, sure, I'm leaving to go on the mission now. I am pretty sure you are, too," said Hailey.

Melanie kept thinking about the conversation as she responded to Miss Daisy. Maybe Hailey was just a tad bit jealous that she was not the mission leader. Melanie put the red telephone down and said, "Coming, Mom."

"Let's get going," Miss Daisy's voice came from somewhere in the background. "Melanie?"

"Coming, Mom," said Melanie.

"I am waiting in the car, Melanie," hollered Miss Daisy, waiting for Melanie.

To tell the truth Melanie was a little bit nervous about the mission but that was only natural. It was her first ever mission. It was a big deal for her and her Mom.

"Sweetie, you coming?" said Miss Daisy again, this time more impatiently. "Yes, Mom."

"Where are we going, Mom?" asked Melanie.

"Well, it's a surprise," said Miss Daisy. "You got your golden envelope with you?"

"Yes," said Melanie. "You're killing me with all the suspense, Mom. Just tell me already," said Melanie.

"Ok, close your eyes," said Miss Daisy. "Moooom," Melanie protested.

"Only if you close your eyes," said Miss Daisy as she opened up the secret console on the car. She briskly typed the escape sequence and "Right There" the garage floor began to recede below the foundation of the house. Melanie opened her eyes in amazement and screamed in astonishment. "This is so cool, Mom, we have a super spy garage elevator right in the middle of our house."

"Well now just you wait," Miss Daisy said as she off-ramped the car and drove straight toward the heavy metal doors at the entrance of the underground tunnels that led straight to HQ.

Melanie could not believe her eyes and ears. She was bang in the middle of a super spy thriller. As they drove in silence, Miss Daisy was still lost in her thoughts, and Melanie was gazing around her in amazement. The tunnel signs whizzed by impatiently. Melanie peered and could only make out bits and pieces of what looked like ginormous moving pictures. This was going to be an adventure of a lifetime.

"Mom," she asked after a bit, "When were these tunnels built?"

"Huh?" Miss Daisy asked

"When were these tunnels built?"

"Oh, several years ago during the war," Miss Daisy responded.

"Well, who maintains them? And how does somebody come in and fix them if something is broken?" Melanie asked

"Doing a world of good is not just the work of spies. There are several other parts of the organization that are just as committed to our cause and believe in the good work that we have done over the decades." Miss Daisy replied.

MDSO was built on the work of scientists, whose gadgets you trained on, soldiers who taught you combat techniques, engineers who built this super complex infrastructure, and powerful members all over the world who want to help the world combat its greatest threats ..." Miss Daisy's voice trailed off.

"Greatest threats ...?" Melanie asked.

"It's not all cupcakes and roses, sweetheart. We train with a purpose. Our purpose is to help maintain peace and combating injustice and evil anywhere in the world. That requires discipline, maturity, and the presence of mind to not only survive but also problem-solve your way through the toughest of situations. This is something I hope your training has taught you well," Miss Daisy said.

"Oh, Mom, I'm ready," said Melanie.

THREE

LONDON, HERE WE COME!

Melanie could still feel the excitement in her bones as she thought about the first trip to HQ. She had come a long way since then, and so had her Mom. *She looked older*, Melanie thought. But what an amazing life she has had, helping so many people and overcoming so many challenges. Melanie watched Miss Daisy effortlessly flip the pancakes and thought to herself that she would definitely want to have as adventurous a life as her mother.

Melanie and Miss Daisy sat at the breakfast table, eating their pancakes and sipping the orange juice occasionally. Miss Daisy flipped open her purse and brought out that dream ticket that every girl hopes for - the ticket to another adventure and possibly a chance to do super cool spy stuff. This was going to be an excellent summer.

"Where are we headed next, Mom?" asked Melanie.

"London, sweetheart. Now, don't gulp those pancakes down; chew your food, please!" Miss Daisy admonished Melanie.

"Oh, come on, Mom, is that why you have been so worried lately? I'm so excited. London is one of my favorite cities in the world! You have just got to stop worrying and give in to the thrill of a brand-new adventure," Melanie said breathlessly.

"Oh, but this adventure looks pretty plain on the surface... I'm worried about the dangers that lurk underneath," thought Miss Daisy to herself.

The next month was a blur, picking outfits, planning the gadget pack, training at HQ and picking up that British accent, just in case you know one had to impersonate a British person. They had the London underground visually memorized and also the suburban map of London. Emergency phone numbers, ground liaisons, safe houses, everything was committed to memory and rehearsed. Every contingency was considered and prepared for.

"Hey, Mom, it's almost time, you know?" Melanie said.

"Yes, I know, sweetie," Miss Daisy said, breaking out of her reverie.

Finally, Melanie and her Mom were spies on a mission in London. The Queen's jewels had been stolen! The thief had successfully overcome all the unbearable, treacherous and impossible obstacles that protected the jewels - Mosquito Mania, Piranha Pool, Laser Lunatics and even the Whirly Whirlpool.

Miss Daisy secretly worried about the safety of Melanie and the other daughter adventurers. A group so skillful, must be very hard to catch and was certainly not acting alone. For the time being she trusted the process and the training and decided to keep her thoughts to herself and not let her fears get the best of her.

There had been whispers of a name and a network that was so sophisticated that it had the wherewithal to execute some of the most daring crimes of the decade. John Adea and EVIL were jointly responsible for decapitating the intelligence network of several nations, crippling the power grid, and holding to ransom several large local and state utilities. Quiet, backroom ransom compromises and a public save-face for local politicians were the typical hallmarks of an EVIL attack. They were responsible for one of the largest networks of organized smuggling of protected animal species and stolen art. A criminal empire that rivaled MDSO in terms of skilled operatives and criminal sophistication.

Miss Daisy had been aware of EVIL and their mysterious leader. But nobody had EVER seen him or knew his name. The criminal empire had its tentacles deep into every government organization. That's how they managed to stay like a nebulous cloud, growing in their power and influence but always staying in the shadows, where no one could lay a hand on them. MDSO had become aware of EVIL as they had caught several low-level operatives and agents who knew nothing about the wider network. Several years of coordination between law enforcement agencies and MDSO ground operatives and field agents have built some sort of CIF (Classified information file) on EVIL. The more Miss Daisy learned about EVIL, the more worried she became. The latest heist had all the signatures of an EVIL operation, and this would be the first time that MDSO and, specifically, Melanie's team would go up against the most formidable opponent that they had ever faced. She was worried, to say the least. Sam and her had decided that they would join the girls on the mission and had taken all precautions with local law enforcement to ensure the girls' safety, but still ... This was EVIL. She just hoped that hubris would lead to a mistake and that, in turn, would lead to the first cracks in the criminal empire known as EVIL.

The girls had been briefed at HQ, but their youthful endeavor perhaps did not entirely grasp the gravity of the situation and the dangers that potentially confronted them. Miss Daisy sighed "Oh to be young and without fear!"

Four groups of moms and daughters were to go on this mission, and Melanie was excited to be working with her friends again. Melanie was super relieved because she was worried, she would have to work with people she did not know at all. But her fears had obviously been unfounded. Melanie was looking forward to adventures with her girl group, and while she would have been a good team player with other agents potentially, it was much more fun with her friends.

"Psst," Melanie whispered to Tanvinisha while they were waiting, "When do you think the others will get over here?" Melanie asked.

"They'll probably be here in 10-20 minutes," Tanvinisha said.

"Yeah, you're probably right," said Melanie.

Just then, Aurora came along and said, "When do you think the plane's going to board?"

Here she is, Melanie thought, *the V.I.P - Very Impatient Person, no 'his' or 'hellos' or even a 'nice to see you guys!'*

"And there she is," Melanie said aloud, in her most annoyed voice.

Esme was dragging about four suitcases behind her, so of course Melanie, Tanvinisha and Aurora offered to help.

After 10 minutes of lugging suitcases across the airport gate, the girls could finally rest. Melanie and the girls were super excited about the trip because they were going to be flying in FIRST-CLASS! Melanie was the most excited. She had never flown first-class before.

They were going to be spying-in-style! just like the super sleuths they saw in movies, neatly cut tuxedos, glamorous dresses, ultra-high-tech gadgets, fast cars and FIRST-CLASS tickets!

The organization they worked for had first-class tickets for its most trusted members. Luckily the girls who got the tickets could sit in seats near each other and play games together instead of getting bored.

When they boarded the plane, they had to wait and the team decided to make a game plan about how they would figure out the criminal's identity and how they would stop him. Just as Melanie took out her laptop to type out a plan that they would follow, Esme shrieked "WHY ARE THERE NO hot towels FLIGHT ATTENDANT!" She pressed the button repeatedly.

They all rolled their eyes, completely embarrassed at the annoying, brattish behavior that Esme was displaying, but after twenty-one missions each being at least a few weeks long they were pretty much used to it. After all, it was a whole 504 days full of tantrums and the rough edges do get smooth over a while.

"It's not my fault that there are no hot rags," said Esme. Tanvinisha was so annoyed that she plugged in her earphones and listened to classical music. The music gave Tanvinisha some sense of peace.

FOUR

THE PLAN AND THE UN-PLAN

"Ok, so it's me again," thought Melanie. Melanie was the lead problem solver, if you had not guessed by now, and the other girls were, well, they were spontaneous, you could say. Usually, Melanie was the one meticulously creating and tracking a plan while the others investigated stuff on their own. As Melanie went typing clickety-clack on the laptop, she suddenly felt grateful. I mean, how many teens get to fly first-class for free on the adventure of a lifetime and catch notorious criminals to boot? "Life," as Melanie would say, "was good."

Aurora was a tad bit disappointed. She felt that if EVIL had committed more crimes before getting caught, more agents would have been assigned to the mission. She was not a very socially outgoing person. It's not that Aurora did not like people (for sure). It's just that she was impatient, which annoyed people sometimes, and they left without getting to know her better. However, her friends were not like that. In any case, she thought she was getting better at expressing herself thoughtfully now.

But little did she know her friends still held on to their earlier views of her. Esme said she appeared to be impatient with others because she was always prepared. Nobody complained aloud, though, considering she always had something for them.

One time when the girls lost their suitcases because someone stole it or the airline had lost it, they were not really sure, and Esme, being Esme, had left her suitcases in the limo. Aurora had completely saved the day by packing an extra set of clothes for everyone. Now that is one prepared girl!

Tanvinisha, on the other hand, loved scary things and was super funny. She also loved horses like crazy and always mentioned things about them. Her lifelong dream was to own a horse ranch one day and ride at equestrian events, but she knew it could be very expensive... she just had to keep working at it.

The girls were hungry. While they wanted to enjoy the benefits of first-class, protocol dictated that at least a couple of meals on the mission had to be MDSO-approved.

The girls all pulled out their compact lunch boxes that could generate nutritious snacks. Not necessarily the best tasting but certainly what the body and mind needed. There were literally teams of scientists, hard at work to make sure that MDSO agents had access to the best nutrition and tech.

This was literally THE BEST part of the job, the cool tech and the gadgetry. Mother Daughter Secret Organization gave all their agents special gadgets like InvisI Spray or the DynaDisguise, that could change the special body suit to any outfit, give them a new hairstyle and a voice texture - a gadget that also happened to be Esme's favorite. Esme was obsessed with all things vanity and beauty. Once, she even went online to see recipes to make your skin shinier.

She put turmeric, curd, and honey all together on her face. It was there for three whole hours, and the whole time, she was just continuously complaining about how much it itches, acting like someone else did this to her.

The Invisible Spray was Melanie's favorite, though. She loved being a fly on the wall and easing into spaces, unnoticed and invisible. It was just the tacky nature of the Spray and the fact that you literally had to shower with a special cleansing solution to get rid of all traces of the Invisible Spray. She remembered the first time she had stood under the Invisible coating station at training and had emerged invisible! What a scare. "For the life of me, what if this is not reversible... OMG, what if I'm left invisible forever?" She remembered panicking until the trainer calmly told her that she could still see her with the Dynavision glasses. It was a hoot later as she washed off the invisible coating with the solution, only to find that there were gaping holes in her body as she stood in front of the mirror. She was goofing around, playing SpongeBob. Ms. Daisy looked at her fondly and remembered the trainer remarking, "It's good she has turned her fear into action and is enjoying the experience."

Aurora's thoughts harked back to her first time at training and how she had met the girls. She had been most certainly overdressed and was going for the boardroom aesthetic while the other girls were more gypsy styled. Some mean ones even called her dressed in the "bored-room" aesthetic. Melanie and Esme were the nice ones, though. They looked past her strict demeanor and talked to her appreciatively. The excitement of the first day of training was quickly shared, and they got down to doing their problem-solving together. It was clear to Aurora from the start that Mel, Esme, and she were going to make a good team. "Three is a good size for a team," she wondered aloud as she nibbled on the healthy snack.

Melanie and Esme stared at her and said in unison, "Not again, Aurora!" "You really have to look at us as the Fab Five."

Aurora rolled her eyes and said, "Yeah, but we are the original three!"

Melanie said, "Aurora, you will always be the one we all count on!" Aurora smiled and secretly was amazed at how Mel had this uncanny knack of saying Just the right thing at the right time.

It was no secret that Aurora and Hailey sometimes had their issues, and Tani was just new. But when it came to the team and looking out for each other, the Fab Five had each other's backs.

Tanvinisha stretched as she listened to the music and took deep breaths to calm herself down. She could barely contain her excitement. The girls had been so nice to her and welcomed her on her first major assignment. And this was London. I mean, O.M.G!

Tani turned around to Esme and Aurora and said, "Guys, don't forget to wiggle your toes and move around." That was Tani for you! Always worried about being physically fit and making sure that the Fab Five was always prepared for their most grueling challenges. The girls hated it but grudgingly admitted that Tani had made them all fitter and made their energy levels higher. They were more formidable opponents for criminals around the world because they were relentless in their pursuits and had the tenacity to close out cases.

As the girls enjoyed the perks of traveling first-class, the organization that they were members of sent a coded message on the secret commspeak channel.

Commspeak was a highly secure channel with the MDSO secret communication network. All the MDSO operatives and agents had bio-implants that allowed them to receive messages wherever in the world they were located. Melanie had seen the complex operations room firsthand during her first visit to the HQ.

"This here is the heart of all our intelligence," said Miss Daisy as she walked with Melanie through the central operations room. "If an enemy were to get access to these networks, the entire organization would be extremely compromised."

"How does it work, Mom?" Melanie asked. Miss Daisy explained the complex encryption technology and the secure bio-implants that allowed messages to be exchanged securely between the agents and HQ.

"Mom, am I going to get one of those bio-implants?" Melanie asked.

Miss Daisy answered the question behind the question and smiled as she said, "No, sweetie, it's not going to hurt. It's like a simple pinprick." Melanie wanted to see how it worked, so she asked Miss Daisy, "Well, if I was an enemy person, and I somehow got into the commspeak network, what would I see or hear?" Miss Daisy said. "Well, why don't we see for ourselves?"

Melanie heard total gibberish and static. She looked at Miss Daisy, perplexed, and said, "I can't hear anything; it's just static and long periods of silence." Miss Daisy smiled and told her to put on the decode headset. She waited excitedly to see the reactions on Mel's face as she heard the commspeak comms. Mel's face transformed instantly, and she could hear her commspeak message crystal clear. "Welcome to commspeak, Melanie! This is MBabel, your commspeak agent. With the bio-implants, you will be able to securely communicate with me wherever you are in the world, and I'll be able to respond. What's more, you and I can have our own secret conversation. Such fun!" This was by far the highlight of the trip for Melanie. MBabel was her new secret friend in the commspeak network. What's even more awesome was that she was able to hear her non-commspeak communications, a.k.a regular, boring, daily stuff, clearly as well. Commspeak would only activate when there was a secret message or when she wanted to communicate with MBabel. Suffice it to say, Melanie felt like a brand-new person after her trip back from HQ that day.

As the commspeak message trickled across to all the girls, their thoughts went back to the first time the bio-implants had made total sense of the gibberish that they had heard without the implants. The content of the message, though, was very alarming, and their thoughts were jolted back to the present time. The message was headlined "of utmost importance and secrecy w.r.t to your mission." The girls hunkered down and started to make notes on their palm-phlets, which, by the way, were another piece of super cool tech from the MDSO labs. They just allowed you to write on your palm with your fingers, and the contents would be changed into notes. They also doubled up as super cool fashionista gloves. And if you wanted to read something you had to request the material on commspeak and you could read it on the palm-phlets. To the ordinary, a.k.a Non-MDSO people would just appear as if the operative was staring at their fashionable gloves.

After the message on the commspeak was done, the girls turned around to activate their commspeak channels to talk with each other without others being able to snoop in the conversation.

"Hey, don't forget to run on your face-ades," Aurora reminded everybody. This was by far the common favorite of all the girls. The face-ades were like these face terraforming masks that made it appear as though the girls were sleeping, whereas, in reality, they were talking animatedly. They just had to be careful about controlling their body movements. So, to the outside observer, it would seem as though the girls were reclined in their first-class seats and just sleeping or reading or whatever face-ade they used, but behind that mask, the girls could be talking without anyone noticing. And, of course, they used it to make faces and play pranks, but they did it in harmless ways.

"This is far bigger than we imagined," Melanie pondered aloud.

"The THRONE, the THRONE! The audacity," Esme said.

"No, not the Throne. I think it was just the jewels on the Throne," Aurora said.

"That's what I heard as well," Tani said.

"Ok, fine, but what's a throne without its jewels, right?" Esme said. "And the Queen's crown jewels too!"

"This does not sound like the work of a single individual. To pull off a crime of this magnitude and to get past all the traps and security levers would require some serious planning," said Melanie seriously.

These were the moments at which Melanie missed Hailey the most, though she hated to admit it. She could just throw out ideas, and Hailey would riff off them, and they would somehow land on an option that they both felt would work. Out of all the possible missions, it was just crazy that Hailey would miss this one. Sure, they had their crazy moments, but they were more like sisters than friends.

Hailey and Mel were tight, but on the outside, it would seem that they were constantly arguing and fighting. They had their first mission together, trained together, and even had the craziest escapes together. Melanie smiled as she thought back to the mission in Paris when the SuperShoes had not worked exactly as planned or, as Hailey put it, "I know I said hover." It was crazy being scared for Hailey and suppressing the humorous tickle at the base of her throat at the same time. It was a blessing, though, that the Invisible Spray had worked exactly as designed." Invisible Hailey " had launched 30 feet straight up into the air, right next to the Eiffel Tower, instead of hovering over the Seine to go over to the footbridge across the river. Mel screamed, and Hailey, invisible, also screamed straight through the air as tourists on the decks and elevators going up the Eiffel Tower looked out in amazement at what they thought was a screaming drone going up into the air. Invisible, Hailey was petrified, but she gathered her wits about herself and had the presence of mind to land slowly and safely. Melanie and Hailey stood there, shaking, wondering at the possible consequences of malfunctioning jetpack shoes.

"Imagine I would have been gasping for air in the outer reaches of the atmosphere," said Hailey

"You are so brave, Hailey, I would not have known what to do. My mind was racing through my options to safely remotely land you. I'm so glad you are safe. What's more you went straight up, nailed a perfect launch so that's a positive.," Melanie said with genuine relief.

Melanie hugged Hailey and said, "Gosh, I wouldn't know what to do if something happened to you."

Hailey said, "I know. Thanks for being there for me always, Mel."

Mel said, "Of course. Even when I hate you and fight with you, I will always be there for you. And I know you will, too."

Melanie and Hailey recounted their adventures to Miss Daisy and Miss Samantha, and the two mothers congratulated them on the special bond that they were forming.

Melanie thought, "Hailey would probably come up with some audacious plan to catch the gang and dismiss good old-fashioned research and spy work as boring." Amazingly enough, or maybe just plain old good luck, the audacious plan would probably work. Melanie chuckled as she thought to herself.

She was still puzzled by one thing though. Hailey had been so insistent that she sent her an email from the flight, letting her know that the team was ok. Oh and the other puzzling thing, she wanted the email sent to the non-secure personal address where, you know, the kids from their school could probably hack into. Mel remembered asking her "That is crazy, we never send emails on the non-secure address."

Hailey said, "Please, I really need you to do this. Just let me know you guys are ok, ok ok ok."

Mel said, "OMG, all right, ok, I'll do it, girlie."

She typed a quick email to Hailey letting her know that she was missing her and that she hoped her tests were going fine. It was almost like Hailey expected, almost wanted to snoop and hack into those emails.

Must be one of those silly challenges Mel thought *I hope Hailey does not inadvertently shine a light on the MDSO secret activities.*

FIVE

SMOOTH OPERATOR

The ultra secret sinister organization that had laid claim to the heist of the century was known aptly as EVIL. MDSO with their various agents and the intelligence gathered over the years had been able to trace back a number of audacious crimes to the organization.

The commspeak message confirmed to the young agents that EVIL was indeed behind the jewel heist.

After the message was relayed, Melanie sat back in deep thought.

First off, it gave her tremendous confidence that MDSO and their commspeak operations had been able to intercept a secret message from EVIL as confirmation. MDSO had been for years trying to infiltrate EVIL but had been unsuccessful thus far.

Melanie said aloud, "I wonder how we intercepted the message."

Aurora replied, "You know I have been thinking about that since we got the message. It must have been one of the super-nerdy hackers sitting in the operations room."

"All those coding classes are part of the training. Now I know why they were useful," Esme chimed in.

"Yeah, among other things, Esme. Hacking is not the only reason why we learned coding," Melanie said. "But I agree, it must have been that super-smart team that must have found a way to hack into EVIL's network."

"Do you think someone actually, I mean, physically infiltrated their organization to get us a secret or some coded key? "Tani whispered.

"Why are you whispering, Tani? It's not like anybody can understand us over commspeak," Esme said, slightly miffed.

"We'll if we can hack into their networks, maybe they can ..." Tani trailed off.

The girls went silent for a second and then dismissed the suggestion as improbable.

But little did they know that at that very moment, EVIL was desperately trying to hack into commspeak and decode the MBabel engine. The super-nerdy team, back at HQ, was already seeing signs of hacker-type attacks on their network and was busy putting protections in play.

The girls took a moment to look around the plane for any suspicious activity before settling down.

Melanie said, "OK, girls, time to decode the rest of the message."

Melanie could not contain her excitement. This was her favorite part puzzling over the clues from an armchair and finding a pattern.

The girls reclined their chairs and watched a movie with kettle corn and a refreshing can of Sprite. Melanie read that the thief had left no clues except a cryptic note that read, "The first of January, the fourth and fifth of October, fifth of March, and first of November."

Melanie figured out the riddle immediately and whispered with excitement! "John the criminal's first name was John! It's because the first letter of the alphabet A the fourth letter of the alphabet D then the fifth letter of the alphabet E lastly the 1ˢᵗ letter again A "His name is John Adea!" Melanie exclaimed; her mind was going a mile a second.

"Brilliant," said Tanvinisha. They all started searching for all the John Adea's in London in the special Mother Daughter Secret Organization catalog for criminals. They did not find anything except that it was an alias for the criminal mastermind of the century and the elusive head of EVIL. Nothing was known about him except that EVIL had claimed responsibility for the most daring crimes in the last decade.

A suave flight attendant came to the girls' area and said, "I hope you young ladies are having a good time. Is this your first time in first-class?"

The girls broke out of their reverie and turned off the face-ades and the palm-phlets. They chattered excitedly and told the flight attendant that this was in fact their first time in first-class and that they were going to London for the first time.

"You must visit the Tower of London- the garden room and the London Eye, of course," said the flight attendant.

Melanie read the name on the badge, "Dane Ojha."

"Well, Mr Dane, we will go there for sure and slay it. We are so looking forward to learning all about the history of the place.," said Melanie.

"Don't miss spotting the black ravens, and do take a picture with the Beefeaters," said Dane.

"How do you know so much about the place?" Melanie inquired.

"Growing up in London in the close proximity of such history has its benefits, you see. I also knew a few people who worked there, of course, a few friends and such." Dane said.

"Wow, that must be nice; I bet you got a few private tours of the tower, sections that are only for the ones in the know," Melanie winked. "We would love to get a more, a more, shall we say, secret tour of the tower," Esme chimed in.

"Bragging rights, you see," Tani said.

"Does the place have a lot of secret tunnels?" Esme asked breathlessly, "And is it true that people were kept hunched in small cages for years and that the narrow stairwells up to the castle wall towers had steps that had irregular heights?"

Dane smiled at the barrage of questions and said, "Tarry Tarry, mind you don't run out of breath and catch a faint there!"

"It's true," Dane continued, "there were many barbaric forms of punishments, including spearing criminals and hanging them in the public square; I bet the walls could tell some stories. The tunnels, though, are an entirely different matter altogether. Secret escape routes in case the royal family was attacked, you see. Some of them were long and led out to the countryside. Now, all of this is the stuff of legend, you see; I personally did not bear any witness to any of these so-called secret tunnels in any of my private tours."

"Ahh, so you admit you did get a private tour! Oh, I'm sooooo jealous," Esme exclaimed. "Do tell."

"Mate of mine I grew up with," Dane said wistfully. "He used to work there and was chums with the Raven keeper as well. Got an inside look into how things work, mind you. Tough job keeping the ravens and training them."

Dane continued, "The towers at the end of the castle walls are interesting, yeah."

"Imagine you are a bunch of graybeards trying to rush up the tower with your spears or bayonets and muskets and such, trying to gain the vantage point of the higher ground, mind you." "It's dark, and your brain calibrates on a certain step height as you rush up, and a steady stream of soldiers behind you are trying to do that same thing. You stumble because the steps are uneven and fall over on the rushing column of soldiers behind you and if you are the beefeater in charge of that tower, you permit yourself a little chuckle as you see the enemy fall literally to its own destruction. Maybe a little nudge to help them along the way," he chuckled.

"Wow, that would make the top of the Morbid Design list," Tani exclaimed.

Aurora suddenly got up and said, "I think Mr Dane, you forgot to give us our hot towels! How much longer do we have to wait? It really is unacceptable!"

Melanie, Tani, and Esme looked at her in shock. Aurora, of all people!

That was rude and very out of character for Aurora.

"We ... all, are you just going to keep standing there gawking or get us our towels?" Aurora persisted.

Melanie tried to interject, "Aurora, I'm sure Mr. Dane here was just about to get us our towels. It's just that we decided to take advantage of his expertise and learn more about the Tower of London.

Aurora looked at Melanie coldly and said, "Yeah, careful they come; I'm sure there is nothing that I could not read up on Wikipedia."

Esme was furious that Aurora's impertinence was making them all look so bad and bratty. "Well, Aurora, if you had been a little more patient with your words and your attitude, we could have persuaded Mr Dane here to introduce us to his private contact."

"Pff private contact... they come a dime a dozen ... hot towels, Please."

The flight attendant looked at her curiously and in silence, "I'm sure, Miss, that I should be able to manage these towels in a jiffy." "Young ladies, If you'll excuse me," and said that he left to the rear of the plane.

The girls turned around in absolute astonishment at Aurora, who was just sitting there smiling. "I'm so furious right now," Esme said.

"Aurora, are you OK?" Melanie said. "I cannot comprehend what just went down. I have never known you to be so, so..." her voice trailed off.

Aurora quickly put the commspeak escape sequence on, and the girls did the same.

"Did you read his name?" Aurora said.

"Yes, Dane, a nice Dane, a helpful Dane, somebody who could have turned the Tower of London experience into a special one," Esme said sarcastically.

Tani looked at her curiously and said, "Why, what were you thinking?"

"Did you read his name, and I mean really read his name?" Aurora asked.

And then it dawned slowly on the girls. Melanie at first, and then Tani and Esme almost whispered excitedly, "OMG!"

"Was that really ..." Esme's voice trailed off as she hesitated to say the name aloud.

"Of course it was, and I had to make a scene to distract him," said Aurora.

"Let's just keep a very close watch on him," Melanie said.

"Yes, and you have my full permission to be as bratty as you want, Aurora," Esme said.

Dane Ojha was an anagram for John Adea.

John Adea observed the four girls from a distance, relying on his honed intuition to sense their affiliation with the organization he had been warned about. This presented an intriguing challenge for him. While arranging the meal trays at the rear of the plane, he reminisced about the close call he had previously experienced. His underestimation of the seemingly bumbling Inspector Marchaud had almost cost him dearly. The inspector's shrewd mind had almost anticipated his every move. Thanks to the mole John had carefully cultivated within the detective's circle, he was able to evade capture.

"That's it," John thought, "I need a mole."

He sent the coded message out on e-comms, the EVIL organization's super-secret communication network, that his agents needed to start identifying and cultivating moles to infiltrate MDSO. John Adea relayed this message to his deputies and wanted a list of prospective candidates ASAP.

Easier said than done, John thought, *let's see who they come up with.*

The foremost concern now was to make a clean getaway from the aircraft without being noticed. Meanwhile, he meticulously retraced his mental steps that led to the audacious heist of the century to ensure that he had not unwittingly left any incriminating evidence besides the clue. With a razor-sharp mind, he methodically analyzes every detail for approximately five minutes. Satisfied that he had left no traces of his identity, he felt confident that he had not made any mistakes. Nevertheless, his intuition warned him that these foes were formidable and posed his greatest challenge yet.

His thoughts rolled back to the present, and he set about executing his escape plan from the cargo hatch.

John Adea was not sure of the identity of the four girls and wanted to confirm his suspicions before making good on his escape, so he thought it might be best to wait to see what the girls would do before putting his escape into action. In fact, he was counting on it.

SIX

HUDDLE

The girls spoke under their face-ades in quick sentences.

"We need to catch him while he is unaware," Esme said.

"He should not know that we are onto him," Melanie said.

"Wait, what if he escapes and knows we are onto him?" Tani jumped in, saying what all of them were thinking but were hesitating to say out loud.

"I know Tani, but we have no choice," Melanie said, "This is an opportunity to catch him like no other. Maybe he underestimated MDSO and is not sure of our identities. We might end up revealing ourselves, but we don't have a choice."

"Well, do you guys have a plan?" Miss Daisy chimed in over the commspeak.

"No, Miss Daisy, we could get some help from you and Sam."

"Samantha ...of course," Esme said.

Samantha, one of the MDSO leaders, and Hailey's Mom of course, observed Dane's actions and admired the neat arrangement of the trays and the great attention to detail. Of course the practicality of carrying such neatly arranged trays on a flight cart was debatable of course. But she had to admit he certainly paid a great deal of attention and was extremely observant.

"Those girls are friends, I suppose," he noted.

"I guess so. They look like total brats to me, acting privileged and such. It's like they think we are working for them, being in first-class and all. Hot rags, my foot. I'm of half a mind to go talk to their parents and get them a nice talking-to."

"Oh, their parents are on this flight too?" Dane asked.

"No, I wish," Samantha responded, "I would not have stood for such impertinence. The girls are unaccompanied."

Samatha thought, *wow, nothing flies past this guy. Maybe he's overly curious.*

As he worked his way through the aisle, making sure the sleeping passengers were comfortable, he eventually brought her a glass of water.

"Here, you look parched."

Samantha took the glass of water appreciatively and murmured, "Thank you, Dane, nice of you."

The last thought that flew through her mind was, "God! What a rookie mistake!" as she slumped into Dane's arms and lay unconscious. John Adea wasted no time and quickly propped her head and shoulder up on the attendant seat. He glanced around quickly to make sure that no one had noticed.

"A small pack of peanuts, please," murmured a tiny voice from the parted curtains.

"Of course," John said. "A moment, please."

This was a spanner in the works, of course. In spite of his best precautions, there was a potential witness. But, of course, he would not be daunted.

"Would you like a smiley face treasure hunt with that?" John asked. "For when you get to London," his eyes twinkle mischievously.

The little girl did not seem to have noticed anything untoward, or she would have raised a hue and cried.

She said, "Yes, of course, mister."

"Ah I know you were one that was up for an adventure. Now, when you land at Heathrow, you are going to have to pass on the smiley face to one of the nice girls over there so that the treasure hunt can continue. That way, you can make some new friends and also enjoy the treasure," he said as he handed her a bag of peanuts and a smiley scrawled on a visiting card.

"Mind you," as he momentarily held on to the card. "Not a moment sooner; otherwise, the clues will vanish; you can hold a secret for that long, can't you? Here's a little sip of water to drink when you are done with those peanuts."

The plan had been put into action.

SEVEN

THE ESCAPE

"Dang it..." murmured John. He had successfully got that pesky flight attendant, Samantha, out of the way. The little girl who had peeked in unannounced was also perhaps safely asleep with the clue card that would hopefully make its way to the girls.

John Adea prided himself on "knowing" things by hook or by crook and, more often than not, by crook. He had grown EVIL into a vast criminal organization that had its operatives in every corner of the world.

For a moment, he felt something akin to pity for these young kids, not knowing the might of the organization that they were taking on. Only for a moment, though. "The toughest enemies are the focused ones, for whom right or wrong is black or white." The gray he could work with...they were malleable... could be persuaded one way or the other, money, threats, or just plain old charm. But these girls, he reminded himself, should be treated as formidable opponents. He wondered at that age how tenacious they would be in the pursuit of the world's foremost criminal.

As he prepared the hatch escape suit his thoughts went back to his own childhood. Tenacity and a certain doggedness had always been his forte. He had big dreams, and he was going to achieve them one way or the other.

His parents encouraged his grit and his tenacity in tackling tough problems. His father was an academic, a professor of Physics at the local university and his mother was a dancer in the local ballet troupe. In a way he was able to apply both art and science to crime.

He was a good student, but his big talent was his nose. He was able to smell weakness in people. He was an excellent organizer and planner and meticulously went about planning and executing every little detail in his plan once it had been formulated. Former operatives who had been caught had mentioned that being a part of EVIL was almost like a college education in the management of crime. Of course, nobody ever met John Adea or knew what he looked like, thanks to the EVIL version of DynaDisguise. Even his voice was unrecognizable in any of the intercepted communications. As the leader of the EVIL organization, it was vitally important that his identity be kept secret and secure. It was an absolute concentration of power at the top, and there were no trusted lieutenants or deputies, only employees who got clear instructions and a detailed plan.

Nobody knew this, of course, but he was unfairly convicted in his first brush with the law. A corrupt policeman was able to plant evidence in his car that proved that John Adea was, in fact, the perpetrator of a local gas station robbery. John Adea protested his innocence, but mugshots were taken, the judge slammed his gavel, and the jury gave its verdict- guilty, John remembered hazily. His talent for organized crime came to the fore in the aftermath of that incident when he decided to avenge that injustice by becoming a thorn in the side of the most accomplished police forces in the world. Every new year, he sent a card to the policeman responsible for putting him behind bars and sending him into a frightened frenzy. John enjoyed the idea of the policeman spending the rest of his life looking over his shoulder, not knowing if this day was going to be his last.

A few daring robberies and money scams gave him enough capital and resources to put together the foundations of an international criminal organization.

He had no dearth of money, and the latest royal robbery was just to prove his daring. His motivation for committing crimes was to enjoy the thrill of being chased and constantly staying one step ahead of the authorities.

He built a vast underground illegal business network that would smuggle and trade in stolen goods, precious metals. His finance pyramid was a complex labyrinth of cryptocurrencies, secret bank accounts and layered organizations that made it impossible to follow a money trail that would lead to him. In short John Adea had to make a mistake for this web of deception to unravel and he was yet to make one.

John stretched out his escape hatch suit and slid down the narrow hatch to the cargo bay. This would be the most daring escape of his lifetime. He left a little card in each of the girls' luggage that said, "Dane's gift, contact 6666, 333, 22, 11 for private tours of London's best spots. The best tower tour- the garden room, the mortar room, the ravens."

John Adea felt confident that they would fall into the trap.

"Begin," he said quietly.

EIGHT

ESCAPE VELOCITY

All mayhem broke loose. The cabin depressurization signal caught all the flight attendants by surprise including the pilots. They frantically searched for the warnings on the panel, but everything was green.

"What do we do?" the pilot said.

"Oxygen masks until we stabilize," the co-pilot quickly responded.

As the oxygen masks dropped, passengers quickly put the mask on.

The girls quickly put them on and took deep breaths into the mask.

And that was the last thing they or any of the other passengers remembered.

The flight from hell had just begun.

Every single person on the plane except for the pilots and John Adea, of course, had taken a whiff of a quick-acting chemical agent that activated on coming in contact with the oxygen and had the instant effect of rendering people unconscious.

John Adea calmly walked back into the main cabin and walked up to the girls in first-class. They seemed so innocuous lying there like that. This was his chance. *Should I just get rid of them?* he wondered.

No, that is not a good idea. I will never know how much they know about my organization and me John thought, *I'll just have to let this play out and let them walk into my trap in a time and place of my choosing.*

His mission was complete as far as this flight was concerned.

The Heathrow landing emergency strip was a flurry of activity. Emergency rescue vehicles and medical ambulances lined up next to the tarmac, where the pilots managed to successfully land the plane.

John Adea allowed himself to be carried out on the aisle stretcher as the rest of the unconscious passengers and the attendants were also carried out. He was taken into a waiting medical van and rushed out of the airport to the nearest hospital.

The girls and the rest of the passengers began to wake up feebly and looked around them in astonishment. The entire scene felt as if it was straight out of a nightmare.

"What happened?" asked Melanie as she tried to clear the fog in her head.

A kind emergency medical attendant replied, "The flight has had the narrowest escape. There was an alarm on the flight, and it looked like the sudden drop in pressure caused most people to blackout. It was a miracle that almost everybody got an oxygen mask on their face before their blackout so that they were able to continue breathing. You are all very lucky that the incident happened close to Heathrow, and the flight was airborne for barely six minutes after the alarms started."

"So we have been unconscious for about six minutes and have landed," Melanie asked. "The last thing I remember is putting an oxygen mask on my face, and it smelled a little funny."

Melanie started, "What about my friends?" she asked in a panic. "Are they ok?"

"Oh, if you mean the girls who are worried about their luggage, hot towels, and their plane gadgets, they are fine and have just woken up as well. There they are," she said, pointing at Aurora, Esme, and Tani. Miss Daisy was standing hunched over a stretcher. Melanie strained her neck to look. Her Mom was listening closely to a person on a stretcher. She peered and saw that the person on the stretcher was Ms Samantha. She did not look too well.

Melanie started to get up from the stretcher to talk to her mother, but a firm hand prevented her. "Now young lady you have had a scare, so as the rest of them, careful how you learn. Best if you lay down a while and let's take care of you. You will be out and hopping in no time, I promise you!" the attendant said.

Miss Daisy hollered from the distance. "Mel, I'm OK, everybody is going to be OK. Don't worry. We'll all go to the hospital, get checked out, and be on our way."

Melanie, thus re-assured, turned over on her side and let the frantic memories of the last six minutes wash over her.

Dane Ojha... "Miss, could you please find out if they found a flight attendant, Dane? I think his name was. He had gone to get our hot towels, and I'm worried about whether he is okay."

"Bless you, child. I'll find out and let you know in the hospital. But I think that they have deboarded everybody. Like I said, everybody was very lucky. Maybe you should drop in a bob or two on the races" she winked.

Melanie needed to clear her thoughts.

The last thing she remembered was the oxygen mask dropping down and everybody putting it on. She recalled looking out frantically to see if Esme, Aurora, and Tani had put on their masks and turned around to look for her Mom. She did not remember anything after that.

"Why would I faint, though?" Melanie thought. Something about that did not seem right to Melanie. "Why did everybody faint?"

The ambulance whizzed through the streets of London, and the hospital was abuzz with police interviewing the passengers and doctors and medical staff working hard, checking out each of the passengers. The girls got their all clear and met with the detectives who took each of their statements in turn, the addresses of their local stay.

Detective Sergeant Tuppence was very professional and kind.

"How are you feeling? None too bad for the experience, I suppose," she said.

Aurora said, "I'm just crazy that my luggage is probably all messed up, and I'll have to spend the time to re-arrange everything?"

Esme rolled her eyes and said, "Aurora, please, you'll slay it again with your packing; we all know that; you'll just take a couple more hours more, that's it. Officer our luggage made it though, correct?"

The girls were worried that the gadgets that they needed for their mission would be lost.

Tuppence replied, "No, that's all squared out. Don't you worry your heads about that at all."

"Now, a penny for your thoughts. I need you to remember anything unusual at all..." Tuppence said.

Melanie said thoughtfully, "It almost seemed planned; why would all of us blackout, and why the alarm if there was nothing wrong with the plane?"

Tuppence said, "That is what we are trying to figure out?"

The girls told her everything they remembered. They all mentioned Dane Ojha and how he was nice to them and had given them nice advice on what to see in London. Detective Sergeant Tuppence took detailed notes and promised them that she would check up on Dane and make sure that he was OK.

"Now, if you girls remember anything, anything at all? Ask your parents to reach out to us immediately, OK?" said the Detective Sergeant Tuppence. She took down their contact information and also the Tower of London Hotel where they were going to be staying.

She wished them goodbye and said, "Hopefully, the rest of the trip will be uneventful, and there will be no more crazy adventures for you."

The girls huddled immediately and began discussing what had just transpired.

"So he went off to get the towels and never came back," Esme said

"This was a very well-organized operation," Tani said.

Melanie said, "Do you guys think it was the oxygen or the masks?" "Well, we can't rule anything out, but my bet would be on the masks," said Aurora.

"Maybe they were laced with something," Tani said.

"Now that is a thought," Esme said. "But that would mean that whoever did this had an inside accomplice, somebody who laced the masks. It would be far more difficult and complicated to deal with contaminating the oxygen tanks."

"I agree," Aurora said.

"Ok, so our theory is that EVIL... I'm thinking this is EVIL. Who did this right?" Esme asked.

The girls nodded, and Miss Daisy also acknowledged over commspeak that it was indeed a good assumption to make.

"But that means that they know of Us, our plans. We should just expect an insane level of prep and challenges from that organization." Tani said.

Melanie said thoughtfully, "Well, if we just concentrated on John Adea, finding him and arresting him, we will have all the information we need to bring the organization down. He seems to be the nerve center of their operations."

Miss Daisy chimed in, "And that girl is our mission. We need to focus on that. Once we have John, the rest of the MDSO teams will work in concert to bring EVIL down. I know you guys are worried and perhaps a little bit scared, but it's OK; I am confident that you will succeed. You have trained hard and are prepared to overcome any challenges that might come your way. Sam is ok, BTW; she is a total trooper but is bummed that the hospital won't release her since she needs to be kept under observation."

Melanie said, "Oh, that's a bummer, Mom we will miss her guidance and experience. Who is going to take over for her?"

Miss Daisy smiled and said, "You know, that's one bit of good news that comes out of this. Hailey will be joining you guys."

"What?" Melanie said excitedly!

"Yay," the girls chimed in unison.

Tani and Aurora looked a little crestfallen.

Melanie noticed and said, "Guys, this is going to be fun. Hailey is the best teammate we could ask for."

"I know," Aurora said, "It's just that sometimes she and I don't get along, you know, like great. Maybe she thinks I'm rude or something?"

"Don't you worry; we all think you are rude, but we love you and would rather have you than anybody else on the team," Esme chimed in.

Tani said, "You know she's not necessarily the most welcoming person like you guys, especially to the new girl, ME. I can hold my own, though, and like her in my own way. I guess we can all find a way to get along and get the mission done."

Miss Daisy smiled to herself, "Little girls, my goodness, so much going on in their heads."

"Mom, I know what you are thinking. So much drama," said Melanie.

Miss Daisy's laughter echoed over the channel. "No, no, I promise you, I was thinking how similar you guys are to how we were growing up, you know, that's all. But jokes aside, you as a team are going to have to find a way to trust and respect each other's abilities and strengths and pick each other up when you fall down. That's what a team is about."

The girls said in unison, "Yes, we will, Miss Daisy. We are the Fab Five, after all."

NINE

LONDON

Detective Sergeant Tuppence had signed their release papers pending medical evaluation. Once the girls got their release papers, they stepped out of the hospital to hail a taxi.

"First things first, I'm really worried about our luggage. The detective said that the luggage would be held at the airport. I guess the gadgets are all fine. I just don't want them to fall into the wrong hands. "Aurora said.

Mel said, "Normally, we would have picked our luggage up from the secret baggage claim inside the terminal. But this time, I guess they moved everything to the regular claim."

Melanie was referring to the time they had traveled to Japan, the economy, of course. After they got off the flight, Hailey and she were met by a terminal attendant who took them to the oversized baggage claim area. They were given security badges and escorted to the controlled area where the MDSO carrier belt was. It was very dull and exciting at the same time, with no secret lair and no tunnels under the terminal, but the awesome part was the breadth and reach of the MDSO organization and the help it was given by all like-minded powers around the world.

Miss Daisy chimed in, "Don't worry about the luggage. Our operatives have already picked up the luggage and taken it straight to the hotel. You guys are excited about the hotel, aren't you? It has a grand view of the tower."

"OMG, that is so cool," chimed Esme breathlessly. "After all the excitement we have had, it would be nice to sip a cuppa tea on the balcony while we figure out the devious endeavors of a certain John," she giggled.

Melanie, Aurora, and Tani all smiled. It was nice to have a light moment after all the tension.

"Will Hailey be joining us there, Miss Daisy?" asked Tani.

"Yes, she will. In fact, I hope her flight has landed safely and she is at the hotel," Miss Daisy said

"Yay! I'm so excited to see her," Melanie said.

"Cabbie," Aurora hollered. "Two cabbies, please take us to the DoubleTree, Tower of London, in double time, please."

Esme giggled at Aurora's effort at a British accent.

"What? "Aurora asked, miffed a little bit.

"Nothing, it's brilliant," Esme said.

"Now never mind, hop on in and I'll deposit your young lot safely to the hotel. Its fancy digs you've got minding you," said the cabbie.

The cab journey was rather uneventful, and they got to see the sights of London, the Thames, of course, and the London Eye.

Miss Daisy walked them into the hotel lobby. As they stood in line, Melanie caught something out of the corner of her eye. She paid no heed to it but just something she registered. The gray-haired man reading the newspaper in the hotel lobby had a two-day old newspaper in his hand. There was the pastry table emanating a fresh coffee and cake smell through the lobby, and of course the cookies.

The gentleman had not turned a page in the 7 minutes that they had been standing in line.

"Could we hurry it up, please? We have had a rather rough day so far, and hot towels, Please!!" exclaimed Aurora rather loudly.

"I thought that was you, Aurie," said a familiar voice. "My God, I have been waiting forever for you guys."

As the girls turned around to look, they shrieked in excitement and hugged Hailey.

"You have to totally listen to the crazy plane adventure we have just had. "Esme said.

"I will; I missed you guys and was so bummed to hear that I was going to miss this mission," said Hailey.

Mel said, "I am so happy to see you, Hailey. I wasn't going to rest until I had called you but it's so good to see you in person. Sam is good btw, so don't worry at all. She is being looked after by the best doctors."

"I know," Hailey said. "Miss Daisy told me already. Thank you all for looking after my Mom."

"So ..." Tani said

"So what?" Hailey asked

"So ... tell us all about it. Is the hotel room really what it's made out to be?" Tani asked.

"Oh, that and more," Hailey said. "Honestly, guys, I don't think that I have stayed in such fancy accommodations since Tokyo. Mel, you and I are roomies."

"Oh, bummer, I thought she was rooming with me," Aurora said.

TEN

THE MOLE

John Adea pondered over his choices. He could use Agent Sapphire as the mole to infiltrate the secret organization that was proving to be a formidable opponent.

"I wonder who the adults are in the organization and what surprises they hold?"

At that moment, John's thoughts were interrupted by the red flickering light, which indicated that a matter of urgency needed to be attended to.

"Come in," he commanded.

Two of his elite agents stepped inside his chamber and stood unsure.

"Well, out with it?" John said.

Agent X said, "Sir, we have some background material on the research you requested for the organization."

"And..." John quizzed.

"Well, Sir, as far as we can tell based on our research, it's a highly secret organization with a very vast underground network of agents. They are a group of mothers and daughters that undertake secret missions and have thwarted some of the more recent attempts we had made before the heist."

Agent IX added, "Their most effective weapons are these schoolgirls who are highly trained and can pass off for a bunch of giggly kids wherever they choose. What they lack in size and strength is that they are made up of highly advanced gadgetry that could rival some of our own. The thing, sir, with schoolgirls is that they can weasel anywhere and, at worst, be treated as a nuisance, never a threat. Their benign presence is what allows them access to the highest levels to carry out their missions.

"Interesting," John mused. "We need more firsthand intelligence if we are to defeat this organization. I'm actually a little upset that they think that they can outsmart ME, the great John Adea, with an episode of "Are you smarter than a 5th grader? Huh?"

John thought quietly, *we need someone that looks like them, talks like them, thinks like them ... best... is one of them!*

"Your new mission is to recruit an ex-agent from this super-secret organization and turn her into one of ours," John ordered.

As Agents IX and X turned to leave, John spoke with a menacing undertone, "Don't fail me. You know I do not tolerate failure."

Agents IX and X left the room and immediately went into a huddle.

"What should we do?" Agent IX said.

"How do we go about finding this random schoolgirl who was a part of this secret organization?" Agent X pondered.

"I guess the first place to start is the scouting section. That's where we vet all our possible new recruits," Agent X said as he started to pace down the corridor of the EVIL headquarters to the scouting section.

He pushed his head through the glass door and made a hand signal to the scouting agent in charge.

"Any interesting chatter or videos pop up on the feed?" Agent X asked.

"Hmm, a few, why do you ask?" the scouting head asked.

"The boss wants a new recruit. A schoolgirl, somebody who can make friends easily, is well trained, and has a mind for some misadventure. Most importantly, somebody we have some leverage on, a weakness we can exploit." Agent IX said.

"Funny, I say," the scouting lead said. "There was a girl just like that today that popped up on the video feed. She was talking about some cool gadgetry and how she used it to hoodwink mall security to play a prank on some bullies from school. She seemed pretty unafraid, only scrambling to hide her phone when challenged by a school warden or something. Almost reminded me of Agent Sapphire when she was younger; she had the same spunk, you see."

"Awesome," the agents said in unison. "We will pay her a visit."

ELEVEN

THE INVESTIGATION BEGINS

The girls were snuggled up in their pajamas in Mel's room. Aurora was pacing up and down the room, thinking furiously while Tanvinisha was busy doing some planks. Mel was lost in her thoughts, and Hailey was watching the TV and the reports going on and on about the plane misadventure.

There had to be inside involvement, "Aurora said. "And it had to be the masks."

"I agree," Mel said. "I have been thinking about it and can see no other way."

"Well, WHO?" Tani asked breathlessly from the plank position. Hailey looked up and said, "Had to be somebody from the maintenance staff, somebody on John Adea's payroll and somebody with enough time to lace the masks."

"Hello, yes, could I please speak to the aircraft operations center? "Melanie was already on the phone.

"Yes, miss, what can I help you with today?" The voice on the other end responded.

"Could we get a staff manifest for all the operations personnel that worked on the plane at the last maintenance stopover for the plane," Mekanie asked.

"Certainly not, ma'am; that sort of information is highly privileged and confidential," the voice at the other end responded.

"Oh well, I'm sorry. I was just hoping to talk to a few of them for a school project on the complexity of airline operations and what a wonderful and extremely technical service the operations staff provides so that passengers can have a smooth journey, sort of like the unsung heroes you see, like the backstage staff for a successful play, nobody ever celebrates them you know. So pretty please, if you could give that to me, I can try and see if a few of them will talk to me about their day," Melanie said.

Wow, she is good, Tani thought.

"Umm I don't know, earlier the police were also asking about the same thing, staff feeling jittery you know with all that's gone down. Some of them are feeling a bit like candy mush right now. Not really up for speaking you know," the operator said.

"I can totally understand; it's just that I have this deadline, and I would, of course, be sure to mention the stellar work of the operations center as well, it being the nerve center and all," Melanie said.

"Let me see, you are such a persuasive young lady and all," the operator said. "Why don't you come by and pick up a list tomorrow evening?"

"Oh goodness me that is so very kind of you, Sir," Melanie said. "I really can't thank you enough."

"Done," Melanie said.

"That was awesome," the girls cried out.

"I wonder who from the police was checking up on the operations staff?" Mel thought.

Melanie wanted to update Miss Daisy and went to commspeak, "Mom, we will have the operations' personnel manifest in the evening tomorrow."

"Wonderful," Miss Daisy said. I want you girls to get that manifest over to me as soon as you get your hands on it. Don't try anything adventurous, we will have some of the senior agents liaise with local police to find out who the inside accomplice was."

"Got it, Mom; Collect and report," said Melanie as she made a wry face toward her friends.

"Well, we know what he looks like for starters..." Aurora said. "I hope Detective Tuppence is able to circulate that description among the police."

The girls were startled by a knock on their door.

Aurora opened the door, and there was a hotel attendant standing there with Melanie's luggage.

"Thanks," chimed Melanie. She immediately opened up the crash-resistant packaging to check on the gadgets.

As she opened the package, a little card flew out. Tanvinisha picked it up and stared at it.

"When did this get here? Wait, was it inside?"

"Yes, it was."

"This is ominous, guys," Aurora said. "It's like he has tentacles everywhere."

"Dane's gift, contact 6666332211 for private tours of London's best spots. The best tower tour- the garden room, the mortar room, the ravens," the card said.

Mel quietly informed Miss Daisy over commspeak about what she had found in the luggage.

Miss Daisy immediately requested central operations to arrange for local security outside the girls' room.

"No problem, madam; Mr. Jones is on-site and will coordinate with the local police to provide additional security."

There was another knock at the door. Melanie peeked through the eyeglass before opening. It was the same gentleman she had seen in the lobby with the 2-day old newspaper. She was not sure whether to open the door when he spoke over commspeak.

"It's all okay, young lady. "I am Jones from the London field operations."

"Mind if I see some ID," Melanie said

"You'd be wise to be taking these precautions, of course," as he flashed the biometric signature approval on the palm-phlet.

Melanie, satisfied, opened the door.

Jones came in and spoke gruffly, "Now you young ones and your safety is my charge and I'd best be keeping a sound mind on me shoulders. That is if you ladies are good at following the words that come out of my mouth, agreed?"

The girls nodded, confused.

"What I mean is that I'll be your security detail and will accompany you everywhere, so you best not be loitering about without a tell-me-who or a tell-me-where, best?"

The girls agreed that having Mr Jones around for their little planned excursion to the operations center was well advised, of course.

"Now show me that little telltale that has all of your little heads in a tizzy."

They showed him the card and explained the anagram and the named clues.

Jones' brow furrowed as he said, "This one's a thief and mischief master at that. He has evaded the law for so long that we are a-weary of ever catching him. But that is a problem for another day; today, we will not be a-weary minding our steps and taking precautions."

"Now rest you up, and I'll keep watch outside. The commspeak will route you to me on Jonesy London; just say SOS if you need urgent help."

The girls nodded and said that they had understood his instructions as he stood up to leave the room. He waited a little and drew the blinds of the window before he left. He made a huge noise and carried on leaving the room, but as he was at the door, he held a finger up to his lips and tiptoed back into the room. He made a signal to the girls to hold up their palm-phlets and perform an audio transmission sweep of the room. As Melanie held her hand under the floor lamp, her palm-phlet beeped. Jonesy motioned her to remain quiet.

"Sorry girls, it looks like it was a false alarm," he said loudly. "Your school trip will not have any further surprises. You can go to the Tower of London as planned and finish writing your report as well. T'was a waster of an evening for me. Your little prank will reach the ears of your well-connected parents, mind you," as he gruffly moved along. "See you, Mr. Jones," Melanie said gaily. "And sorry if our little scare bothered you." The girls quietly tiptoed outside.

Jonesy asked quickly, "Was all your conversation over commspeak?"

"Not all of it," Aurora replied. "We were talking to each other normally, not over commspeak."

"Well, you had a bug in your room, and in the other rooms, too, I would assume. Every chat that was not over commspeak was probably heard by whoever bugged your room. Just safe to assume that all your communication was compromised. I'll run a scan to quickly check where the bug is transmitting to and if we can hone in on the location. With a low-power bug like that, it has to be on the hotel premises. Meanwhile, you stay put and watch a movie or something."

Mr. Jones called Miss Daisy over commspeak and updated her. Miss Daisy sighed in exasperation, "Training 101 girls!" but it was probably the adrenaline from the days' events that led the kids to miss this. Nonetheless, Miss Daisy expected better,

Mr Jones called back two hours later to report with an address in London of an off-duty front desk operator to who the bug receiver was traced.

That should take care of that.

Detective Tuppence broke down the door of the seedy neighborhood flat that the address pointed to. A thoroughly underdressed young man with a pack of chips and a phone in his hand stood aghast as Detective Tuppence handcuffed him and took him to the police station for interrogation.

This was going to be a long night as she settled in with coffee, and the hotel clerk was booked in.

TWELVE

RECRUITING OPERATIONS

Agents IX and X scoured over the files

"What about this one?" Agent IX asked.

"No, her Mom and dad have both served on a jury, likely a strong set of ethics." Agent X said. "OK, missed that, " Agent IX chimed.

"What are you so cheerful about?" Agent X demanded petulantly.

"We are on death row if we don't find this elusive super-agent."

"Well, might as well enjoy the ride; I thought we had her, but no information at all on our high bar prospect. "Agent IX said,

"Moreover, an agent like that should be hard to find, don't you think?"

"Back to it then."

The agents went back to poring over their files.

"I'm going to grab a brain booster; I think I need it and a fresh perspective," Agent IX said.

"Do you want anything?"

"No, don't think so, but I agree we are missing something; we have looked at modest academic records, ethical shifty-sands, dicey family dynamics, possible ex-agent, low to medium profiles, nothing that attracts too much attention ..." her voice trailed off. "You know, maybe we have been looking at this wrong. Any girl who gets rejected like that surely has a chip on her shoulder and wants to prove the world wrong, and the best way to do that is to be the center of attention. I'm going to modify the criteria and run the search again."

"Nawh, it's going to take another couple of hours. Shouldn't we just finish the list first?"

"I've got a hunch about this, just trust me," Agent X said.

The blue scrolling circle on the screen started its crawl again.

"Ok time to grab that booster shot and maybe get a couple of hours in the oxygen chamber as well." Agent X said.

Meanwhile, what Detective Tuppence thought was going to be a long night was rather quickly and summarily concluded. The hotel clerk folded quickly. He had been asked to set up the bug just a couple of hours ago by two agents in black suits who actually showed him government IDs and said that this was part of an international mission. They naturally swore him to secrecy and assured him that his service to his country would not go unnoticed. He was to record the audio on a device and drop it off at a mailbox.

"So, did you do it then?" Detective Tuppence asked.

"No, I was not able to, not today's recordings anyway," "I put yesterday's recordings in the mailbox."

Ok, so that is a bit of a finger in the pie, Detective Tuppence thought.

"You will now serve your country," Tuppence declared loudly. This situation presented an opportunity to work her way up the spider web of the EVIL organization.

"No, nothing to be worried about, but I wonder if the girls could record some audio for me." she said softly over the phone.

The screen stood frozen with a picture. The girl in the picture had an outstanding academic record, every single detail in her resume marked her out for academic success. There were those two missed summers though, ostensibly vacations but no official records of her being present in those destinations at that time. Her family did not look rich enough to have private transportation. So what was she up to in those two summers?

Curiously, she became an academic and athletic overachiever after those two summers, the same school as one of the girls in the "other" organization. It was not really the friends-friend dynamic with the other girls, but they definitely knew each other.

In short, was this the one they had been looking for?

Agents IX and X stood staring at the screen, unable to believe their good fortune. "Well, that was a masterstroke," Agent IX said. "Fancy you thought of that?"

"Let's pay her a visit." "What do we call her?"

"You mean in code. I like Storm."

A couple of flights later, the agents found themselves in a quaint little suburban neighborhood south of San Francisco.

Their hunch had proved right. "Storm" was active on the underground hacking network and had agreed to meet them. The agents had not offered her too many details but just an interesting freelance opportunity that might align well with some of her other non-academic pursuits. "Storm" was savvy enough to know that the people reaching out had done their background research and would only seek to meet because they probably knew about her MDSO past.

"Storm" and the agents met at the coffee shop.

"A cold brew with cream, I presume?" Agent IX asked.

Storm nodded and stared keenly at Agent X in front of her. With strong arms and sinewy muscles, she seemed athletic and dangerous if needed. What was remarkable was how easily she fit into this idyllic suburban setting, even whipping out her phone to small talk with the yoga teacher.

"So," Agent X said, after putting her phone back, "Now that you have sized us up? "What do you think about our offer?"

"Let me see, you want me to go up against MDSO, break all the loyalty and trust with my friends and potentially run afoul of the law?"

"Now, really, the circumstances of your exit were less than ideal, yes?"

"Yeah, after my injury, I thought they would rehabilitate me back into missions, but I was summarily retired! Mind you, it was a fun gig. But the injury had healed, and they simply would not give me another chance. Be awesome. Behind a screen, they said, "Huhh," "Me, I was their top operative; I was born for field action, not to sit behind some screen to hack away. I ran a single renegade mission, but the fools did not see that I was trying to help them, and a couple of psych evals later, they retired me. But why am I telling you all this? You already know."

"So yes, if I can have my revenge and show them what they are missing, then yes, I'm in."

"Good, we'll do this the good old performance scholarship way. If you need us to pay your parents a quick visit, we can do that too."

Storm said, "No, they have been through the routine before and will bite on the scholarship training program charade, so yeah, pull that off, and I'm on board. Standard three weeks of accelerated training, I think? I should be able to ramp up to training levels pretty fast."

"That depends on if you are a model student." Agent X pursed her lips.

"I don't believe that you honestly have any doubts about my ability. So I'll take the last comment as one of sincere concern for my well-being," as Storm sauntered off after setting her cup down on the table.

Agent X and IX were very pleased with the outcome and couldn't wait to apprise John of their success.

THIRTEEN

A MAZE OF DEAD ENDS

John and Melanie quickly made their way to the operations room and asked to see the director. Melanie had her notes book and school folder prominently jutting out of her backpack to make sure everyone knew she was at school.

"So you are the young lady who wants to interview our maintenance personnel?" he asked.

"Yes, sir, and thank you so much for agreeing to meet with me,"

"Here is a list of questions that I plan on asking them," she offered a typed-up list of questions.

"Well prepared, I see," the director said as he squinted over the list.

"Just a few conditions, though: you will have to interview them here at the office and only during their breaks. Do you think you can do that? I assume your dad will accompany you here? About a couple of hours each day between shifts, I think I should do it."

"Thank you, sir," Melanie gushed. "I will send you a copy of the report once it's done."

"So it was you who did the maintenance checks for the plane the last time it took off?" Melanie asked the operations team that was seated languidly in front of her.

"Yep, sure was, and lucky for you, we flew in for our shift with these new planes to London. Mind you, no first-class travel though, treated like cattle… us folks, what would I give …" the girl's voice trailed off.

"No, I mean, I'm super thankful that you are sharing the time between shifts with me for my report. So who does the general cleanup and the maintenance of the toilets and the other stuff for hygiene, you know?"

"Depends on the roster; it was Deandra, I think, that day."

Deandra looked up lazily, "Yeah, it was me," she drawled.

"Cool. How long have you been doing this? What is the best part of your job? Do you think?"

Deandra looked at her, surprised. "It's all a drag, I s'pose. I mean, I'm cleaning, what could be exciting about that? But man, sometimes people leave behind the grossest stuff: nosy napkins and crumpled bottles. I just think it would be nice, yeah, if they left it clean for the next person I s'pose."

Melanie asked, "Do you also take care of the overhead bins?"

"Yeah, I do have to, although I have help."

"What about the oxygen masks? Who ensures that they are in working order? I've always wondered what would happen if I pulled the mask in a crisis and it didn't work; gosh, what a terrible panic I'd be in," Melanie said.

"Oh no, that is not a part of the regular cleaning operations. It's done once every year, I think, and at the hub. It's like a month-long exercise."

"Ahh," Melanie said resignedly.

Melanie thought hard about her options as she spoke with the operations team. The chemical treatment was designed to activate when coming in contact with oxygen, but if it was not the masks, then what was it? *What was common to all the passengers?* she thought as she racked her brain.

She took a small break to jot her thoughts down in her notebook.

1. The chemical was activated in contact with oxygen.
2. It had to be something that all passengers used.
3. The timing of the activation had to be planned, which meant that the emergency was also triggered and planned and was not a sudden random occurrence. - *Note to self - follow up on this lead as well,* Melanie thought.

Melanie racked her brains to see if there was any follow-up question that she could ask.

"You know that flight? The one that made an emergency landing? Must have been crazy that day?" She casually remarked.

"Don't you even get me started, such a wild ride. I don't think I have seen so many emergency vehicles pull up at such short notice."

"Yeah, thankfully, the sanitization crew was super-efficient in cleaning up the plane immediately after. It was so hot during takeoff that we had to dip into the reserve fresh towels since folks were so sweaty during takeoff."

A thought triggered, and Melanie said, "You are right. It was an unusually hot day, and it seemed like the flight air conditioning was working extra hard."

"Oh, were you on that flight?" a sleepy operator asked. Melanie hastily said, "Oh no, just what I read in the newspaper."

Melanie thanked them all and went back to the hotel taxi with Mr Jones.

Once they were in the taxi, they switched to commspeak, and Mr Jones said, "Rather curious, don't you think?"

"Yes, OMG, it was not the masks, but it was something that all the people used that only activated in contact with oxygen! I'm actually thinking the towels were laced with the chemical that knocked us all out!"

"Yes, that was obvious, of course," Mr Jones said. "I was thinking of this operator who was pretty much sleeping the whole time but woke up when you mentioned rather sloppily about the day being hot and the flight air conditioning being inefficient."

Yes, we should definitely track that guy, Melanie said "but what about the towels do you think the metropolitan police could chase that down?"

Mr Jones said, "Afraid that's a dead-end, young lady. It's a complete maze of supply chain companies that provided those disposable towels. Very hard to pinpoint where the towels were contaminated."

"Ok, well, what about the operator that got arrested? Was the detective able to find anything from him?"

"Oh yes, he folded, alright! But he was a very low-level operator that received instructions and payments in cash through dead-drop sites, so no, nothing useful there."

"Ahh," Melanie leaned back, disappointed. Every clue in this case was leading to a dead-end.

"Gosh, this is so frustrating," Melanie said

"What is?" Mr Jones asked.

"Well, if you already knew about the towels and the operator, why accompany me on this sham interview?" Melanie asked.

"It's what's called setting a cat among the pigeons. That operator, if my hunch is right, will report to his higher-ups about the little Q and A we just did. We have just shaken the tree. Let's see what falls out."

"Oh, I see," Melanie said.

"Patience, young lady, patience!"

FOURTEEN

THE PRE-AUCTION

The pre-auction site was full. There were private collectors from all parts of the world with their commercial agents.

John Adea motioned for the pre-auction to begin. The bidding was swift and furious, and everybody wanted an invitation to the actual auction to be held at a secret location.

John Adea congratulated the winning syndicates and also signed the insurance claims to the jewels with the guarantee of replacing them if they were ever to get robbed.

The syndicates agents were impressed! What gall! The guarantee replaces the irreplaceable jewels! That's why John Adea was John Adea, and his guarantee was better than any other insurance.

John Adea, too, lived for this adulation rather than for the small fortune he had just made. Sure, the money would come in handy for research and his next exploits. But this recognition, this appreciation, was what made him pull off these daring heists.

A small niggle of doubt nonetheless remained. He did not like his hand being forced. Since he received the report of the MDSO agents and specifically one of "those girls" snooping around the operations team asking about the towels, he wanted to make sure that the jewels were sold before they were tainted "hot."

The jewels were still in his secret EVIL HQ location. As he ran his fingers over them, he wondered if he should renege on the deal he had just approved; he smiled as he thought to himself, *what would this collector do anyway? Go up against John Adea? Huh?*

He quickly put that thought to rest because the reputation that John Adea had was the most sacred thing to protect. He knew that these collectors bought from him because their reputations would go untarnished and because of his "EVIL" insurance policy. That could not be compromised at any cost.

Agents IX and X were summoned and given the dual charge to the three-way code that was needed to unlock the safe where the jewels were safely stowed.

He asked them where they were on the recruitment of Agent Storm.

Agent IX replied, "She is a natural, but I have doubts about her temperament. She seems very impulsive."

Agent X chimed in, "I think she is a good fit for the situation. Motivated by revenge and a desire to prove herself to be the best, she has some utility for the time being."

"Well then, the time is now, as the jewels are being transacted, I need a distraction," John instructed. Onboard her into the program and into their lives.

John Adea said, "One final thing: I don't tolerate mistakes. This was the heist of our lives, and I have a special place in mind for the exchange. Make no mistake, I will be ruthless in extracting punishment if anything, any single thing goes wrong."

FIFTEEN

BUSINESS AND PLEASURE

The girls had decided to take the day off and go sightseeing in London. They spent the day marveling at St Paul's Cathedral and the smaller chapels of St Michael and St George.

"Esme, don't lean over so much you might just fall off," Aurora giggled.

"Fancy, Aurora cracked a joke," Esme said. Everybody laughed out loud as they took pictures.

Mr Jones's voice drawled pleasantly over commspeak as the girls huddled into listen.

"So we've shaken the tree, and something has fallen out. There have been reliable reports that the jewels are being actively transacted. Which means EVIL will be in a state of high alert, also means that you guys have to be on the lookout for any suspicious activity.

The girls continued to behave normally and take pictures, but they were on high alert. Melanie noticed that two men had been on their tail. She announced loudly, "Girls, we have very little time. Do you think we should start to walk toward the tower now? After all, we do have a private tour that was promised."

They slowly made their way up St Paul's churchyard and then to cannon street. Melanie made sure that they stayed together as a group.

"Tani not too far ahead? Please."

Esme stopped a little to open up her vanity case and flicked open her mirror and saw that the two men were still on their tail. They quickly hushed over commspeak.

"Mom, Sam? You guys there? we think we are being followed. Mr Jones?"

Nothing radio silence.

A few seconds later, "Mr Jones here, those are not our personnel. You need to get to a safe place. Find a coffee shop or something and stick together. BTW where are Ms Daisy and Sam? we have not heard from them since this morning?"

Melanie and Hailey were worried, so they walked into a small coffee shop and ordered some pastries.

"Mr Jones, we were trying to get them on commspeak as well, but they did not respond. Sam was feeling well the past week. Maybe she had to make a dash to the doctor, and my Mom accompanied her?"

"Not very likely, my dear. They are seasoned agents who know the importance of daily check-ins. If they have missed it, it is certainly not voluntary."

"Wait, I know. Could we use the commspeak proximity meter or their palm pellets to track their location?"

"Now that's a thought, give me a minute."

After about a minute of static, "Found them. For some reason, they are in the Tower of London." "Both of them?" Hailey asked.

"Yes," Mr Jones replied, "And they seem to be moving at a much faster pace than walking. Now you stay put though, till I send some officers there to escort you back to the hotel."

Melanie thought that if her Mom and Ms Sam were in trouble, then they would not have a single second to lose. She whispered over commspeak, "Girls, we need to track and find them now." The girls nodded in agreement.

"So what's the plan," Tanvinisha asked. "Do we put on the Invisible Spray?"

"OMG, that is like the best part of my job," Aurora said.

"That is a good idea, Tani; we should take out the Invisil Spray and maybe also use the Super Shoes to get to the tower quickly," Esme said.

Hailey and Tani rummaged around in their backpacks with a crestfallen look.

"We didn't pack the Spray or the shoes," they cried.

"Don't worry, I have spares for both, but the problem is I have one Spray and one pair of shoes extra," Aurora said.

"It's a big risk. One of us will have to stay behind," Melanie said.

"Hailey, use my shoes and my Spray. Tani, use the spare one from Aurora ", Mel directed. "I will stay behind and coordinate with Mr. Jones on commspeak. And please, for goodness sake' girls, watch the time; you know the Spray wears off in 30 minutes, and the shoe's batteries last about an hour at the most. If you guys can't get in formation, then huddle together someplace and don't take any unnecessary risks. I'm sure Ms Sam and Mom are fine."

Hailey could tell Mel was worried since she called Miss Daisy's Mom. She rarely did that. She was worried, too, as her Mom had gone radio-silent.

The girls went to the back of the restaurant and sprayed themselves and their bags and shoes.

"Godspeed," Tani giggled. Aurora said, "Really, Tani, not the time!" "Let's focus on tracking Ms Sam and Ms Daisy in the tower."

Mel put on the face-ade, and it appeared as though she was staring silently into space. But she mumbled instructions over commspeak.

"Ok time yourselves, you should be at the Great Fire Monument in another 15 minutes. Then onto St Dunstan in another 5 and enter through the Traitors Gate. As the Spray starts to wear off, I want you guys clustered inside. I will ask Command Ops to track your shoes.," Melanie said.

"We got this, Mel, don't be worried; we will find Ms. Daisy and Ms. Sam," Hailey said. "Right, girls?"

Aurora, Tani and Esme put their invisible hands on Mel's shoulder and started their hover shoes. The four of them hovered with their shoes about 6 feet in the air, checked the vital boot up-signs. Once they confirmed that the shoes were good for an hour, they checked in over commspeak. "Aurora is a go," "Esme is a go," "Tani is a go," and "Hailey is a go."

They increased their hover to about 18 feet and leaned forward on their shoes as if they were hoverboards; they fell into formation with Tani leading since she was the newest, Aurora and Esme flanking her, and Hailey bringing up the rear.

"Good luck, girls," Mel whispered.

As they sped off on their hoverboards, Melanie checked in over commspeak. "Mr. Jones, the girls have gone to check on Ms Daisy and Ms Sam on their hoverboards, and they are flying invisible. They will take side streets and flank tall buildings wherever possible to avoid detection." Mr Jones sighed, "I knew the Fab Five would not sit idly by. Ask them to check in when they get to the tower, Traitor's Gate, is it? It has the guard change in another 30 minutes."

"Read our minds, Mr. Jones," said Hailey.

Melanie sat inside the coffee shop, wondering how to shake off the two men who had been tailing the girls. They would certainly get suspicious if they had noticed that five girls had gone in and only one had come out.

"Mr Jones, I have to draw their attention. Is the backup close by?"

"They should be in the vicinity. Don't worry. You are safe."

Melanie stepped out as if she was taking a breath of fresh air. The London air was quite bracing right next to the Thames.

She looked idly at a couple of flowers on the fence posts, as if admiring them, all the while scanning the surroundings for the two men. And sure enough, at the newsstand opposite the coffee shop, they stood innocuously. Melanie was absolutely sure that these were the same men who had been tailing them. She wondered if she should lead them back toward the cathedral.

"Agent IX, five of them went in, and only one stepped out. Should we make contact and bring her in?"

"No.." Agent IX said thoughtfully. "I have another idea in mind."

"Keep an eye out for the other four." They must be up to something. There was no way they could jeopardize the rendezvous at the tower. There already had been reports of a slight intrusion at the tower. John Adea would be furious if the meeting at the tower was in any way jeopardized.

Time to mobilize our secret weapon, thought Agent IX as she dialed into the secret comms.

Melanie loitered for about 15 minutes and then checked into commspeak.

"Girls, Are you at the first milestone, The Great Fire Monument?" She asked.

After some static, Hailey's voice drawled in pleasantly, "Yes, Mel, we are running about one minute behind, but we are almost there. We fell out of formation for a bit."

Melanie said, "Ok, guys you will be cutting it close but will make it there, I'm sure."

Melanie wondered why her Mom and Ms Daisy were at the Tower of London and why they had gone radio-silent.

"Sam? Sam? "Ms Daisy whispered. "Can you hear me?"

"Barely Dee, there seems to be some sort of jamming interference going on, but I think our encryption will hold. My palm-phlet is warning me of a possible intrusion attempt on the secure channel, which means that the adversaries here are on high alert," Ms Sam replied.

"I think we should have gotten Mr. Jones and the girls involved," Ms Sam said.

"I know but we literally had to react as soon as the meeting information was received by us. There was no time at all," Ms Daisy sighed.

"Well, it's the usual coterie of tourists and a bunch of school kids on tour; nothing amiss here," Ms. Sam said.

"Wait, my palm-phlet just went silent..." Ms Daisy said.

"OK, on the high alert then, that means we are off the grid now and reliant on local comms," Ms. Sam replied.

"Where did the informant say the meet was? "Ms Daisy asked.

"Blundeville Tower," Sam said, "But you know I did not see it on the tower schematics."

"Man this better not turn out to be some wild-goose chase." Ms Daisy replied. "Although I think something weird is upon us since there are so many intrusion attempts."

"Sam, Sam, did you say Blundeville Tower?" Ms Daisy asked.

There was just static on the channel.

"Sam, Sam, are you all right? If you can hear me, the Blundeville Tower is known as the White Tower now," Ms Daisy asked. "Sam?"

"Sam, respond with your code name."

"Sam, I am activating the Aite protocol," Ms. Daisy said.

Daisy stood in the mortar room in the White Tower and watched a thin stream of tourists walk through the room, muttering a steady stream of exclamations over their audio guides.

She asked a particularly elderly lady, "Madam, may I bother you for a minute, please?"

"Time has a yard on all of us, even the fleet-footed, so yes, you have but a minute," the lady smiled back.

"Oh, thank you, can't be bothered to be getting any more yards on these creaky old knees of mine," Ms Daisy chuckled.

"I wanted to ask you if I could perhaps borrow your cell phone for a moment." Ms Daisy asked.

"Oh, but sure, they a but a yard or two too fast for me while walking and while talking. Fancy them telling an old fossil like me what it was like in the old days," the lady guffawed, handing Daisy the cell phone.

"Take your time with it, and if the fog settles, share a word with an old lady on what it all means. Careful how you go."

Daisy took the phone, thanked the old lady, and quickly settled into a quiet corner. She put on the face-ade, making it appear she was listening intently to whatever was playing on the cellphone app, but she was furiously plugging in a modular transmitter from the palm pellet. She knew that the comms would not be secure and would likely give away her location, but she was sure that the message would be intercepted, and help would likely arrive.

"Aite Protocol activated. It's time to check the grades for the student essays on the history of the Tower of London," she said. And then broke the transponder.

"Here you go did not work for me at all. It wasn't the chatter, just a bad audio set, I think," Daisy said as she handed the set back to the old lady.

"Oh, there you are I have been looking all over for you, Auntie George," a smartly dressed young woman exclaimed.

"My word, I do believe she is addressing me. I'm getting really fog-headed now," the old lady exclaimed.

"Let's go, then, unless you want to spend all day here," the young woman said rather testily.

"Oh my dear, I'm sorry I must be a light-headed from all the walking, but who are you?" the old lady said.

The young woman said "Now, really Auntie George, if that is by way of a joke then it is in really poor taste." Daisy stepped in and held the old lady by the arm, bent over to check the temperature on her forehead. As Daisy did she felt a little prick on her neck.

SIXTEEN

THE RESCUE

Melanie was in shock. She was sure she had seen an apparition.

No, it could not possibly be, she thought.

Donning a stylish white coat with black symmetrical borders and smartly tailored pants, Crystal waved enthusiastically to her. "Oh my God, is that really you?" she screamed.

Crystal ran toward Melanie, who, unsure of how to respond, stood rooted to the ground.

She grabbed Melanie by the shoulders and shook her, "OMG, how very cool, how so very slay to see you here, Mel!"

"Sure," Melanie shook her head. "I'm sorry, I was just so shocked at seeing you here; I did not know how to react."

"Oh my God, you have to tell me all about it. I'M SO EXCITED. Wait, lemme call Mom and tell her. Crystal blurted out breathlessly. "Oh wait, you simply have to meet my exchange program partner, Donnie." "She has a cute accent and all; you'll love her," "Hey, Donnie, come here. I want you to meet like the smartest, coolest friend I have ever had," Crystal said rapidly, breathlessly.

"Crystal, I'm so excited to see you, really, and Donnie, nice to meet you too!" Melanie said.

"Wait, who are you here with?" Crystal asked.

Melanie hesitated, "Well, Hailey ..." as her voice trailed off.

Crystal stood in silence for a bit. "You know what, it's ok! I know we did not part on the best of terms, But I felt like I was misunderstood by Hailey for a bit as well, and God knows she did not make it easy for me to understand her, and it's totally cool that I'm not your BFF anymore, its ok, really "But what I am right now is really really glad that I ran into you and I refuse to let you out of my sight for a single second," Crystal said happily.

Melanie bit her lip and said, as precious seconds passed, "Crys, something's up, and I need to go to the Tower of London. Mom was there as well, and we were supposed to meet up. She would get worried if I was late. She promised to send a taxi, which is what I was waiting for when I saw you?" Melanie thought silently, *if I ever needed an adult to show up, I should be right about now.*

Crystal said, "It's curious; that's where Donnie and I were headed, and I have a taxi waiting unless you want to," Crystal winked. "Some old-time adventures."

"Hush Crys, you know we are never supposed to talk about that, and this is a vacay, so yeah, none of that, please, "Melanie said. "Let's go to the tower."

"Yay, just like the old times!!" Crystal said.

"So how's the new school? I mean you just disappeared after our last Vacation together?" Melanie asked.

"Yes', 'Crystal said, "I did. I just was so bothered by Hailey and your new friends, I guess, taking up all that space that I could not focus on studies, our friendship, and our secret missions. I just wanted to get away from it all. Plus, I think everybody sort of lost confidence in me."

"I'm so sorry if that's how you felt, Crys. That is not true at all. We were all rooting for you to succeed. After all, you were one of the first members. Mom always felt that you were the most talented of us all." Melanie said.

Crystal slowly breathed and twiddled the buttons on her coat. "It sure did not feel like that when I was called to HQ and told that …" she trailed off.

"Anyway, all that training helped me recover from the knee injury I got. I even go cross-country skiing these days. Anyway … I'm fine now. You know, I think I want to be a lawyer," Crystal said.

"That is super slay." Melanie added.

"What is going on with you? This is not the Mel I used to know. Here I am going on about what I want to do and you have nothing to add? How have you been, how's Miss Daisy, cmon spill," Crystal asked, miffed.

"To tell you the truth, I have a lot on my mind right now," Melanie said. "Right here would be just fine," she said to the driver.

"Crystal here is my hotel address. Let's meet tomorrow, will you promise me you will come? Is your Mom here with you?" Melanie said.

"Well, that is odd. Are you sure you want to get off here? Yes, I will come tomorrow. I'm here as a part of a student exchange program from my school. So I will request one of the group leaders to come with me. You take care, Melanie and it was good seeing you!" Crystal said.

Melanie said her goodbyes and went to a quiet, unobtrusive corner. She frantically pinged Hailey and the others.

"Where are you guys?" Mel asked. "My palm-phlet is reporting an Aite protocol activation from the tower. Is that you guys, or is that my Mom?"

Silence. Melanie breathed deeply and thought to herself, *calm down it's just a temporary glitch perhaps. The guys are ok and my Mom and Ms Sam are ok as well. They are trained for precisely this sort of emergency.*

After some static, Melanie tried again, "Guys, if you are able to hear me, I'm near the tower entrance and am planning to go inside; let me know your coordinates."

"Mel, Mel," a whiff of a whisper.

"Mel."

"Yes, Hailey? OMG, are you guys ok?" Melanie said.

"No, we almost got our covers blown, but we were able to make an unseen entrance. The hover shoes are practically useless now, so the exit will have to be the traditional way." Aurora said.

"Exit, what do you mean? What have you guys found out?"

"Mel, we have some bad news. Just as we were entering, we got an Aite activation and saw some medical ambulances pull up. Apparently, two ladies fainted in the mortar room. The mortar room was also where the Aite was activated from. We went there but could not find any trace of Miss Daisy or Mom," Hailey said.

"Don't worry," Aurora said. "Hailey, Mel, we will find them."

"We got comms out to Mr Smith, and he said that the high alert signal had been received. And that they were tracing the ambulances. Nothing yet." Tani said.

"Ok, my mind is not working right now," Hailey said. "It feels like we should be looking for Mom and Miss Daisy."

"Mr Smith asked us not to as he got the MDSO operatives tracing them from HQ," Tani said.

"Yeah, well, it's not your Mom," Hailey said.

"That's not fair, Hailey," Tani and Aurora exclaimed.

"I know, I'm sorry, just that I feel pretty helpless right now," Hailey said.

Mel said slowly, "There was something they were chasing in the tower, and we need to go find it. They would want us to do that. This is our training, guys. We owe it to them."

"Ok, I will rendezvous in five mins at the mortar room."

The pamphlet took Mel right to the mortar room, where the other girls were waiting. Hailey hugged Mel and whispered, "I'm so sorry and so worried."

"I'm sure they are going to be fine," Mel said.

SEVENTEEN
THE AUCTION

John Adea surveyed the room. The grandiose setting and the resplendent furniture of the imperial era seemed like a fitting backdrop for the auction. He was in disguise of course as a member of the tower staff.

It's rather inconvenient, he thought that the MDSO senior operatives had shown up when they were at the Tower. Surely, there was a leak in his organization.

I will have to plug that, of course, permanently, he thought.

The countermeasure by Agent IX had proved successful, and the old lady was minor collateral damage, nothing a nice gift basket couldnt resolved, he chuckled to himself.

The two senior operatives had been whisked away, and hopefully, the remaining agents had gone chasing after them.

"Hope, hope's got a yard or two on the best of us," John said aloud.

"I want confirmation that the subterfuge worked. These agents were not to be terminated. They are to be interrogated, and the extent of their knowledge about EVIL needs to be determined. I want to know everything that they know. Use the neural agent to read their mind. I want the experience to be pleasurable and not painful. They should open up their thoughts to me as if the system were their closest confidante.

"And failures will NOT be tolerated," John Adea signed off with a sinister laugh.

As he mopped the grandiose marble floors, John Adea got thinking. Did this secret spy organization actually have a leg up on EVIL? Thankfully, he had a backup plan and a secret weapon. Storm had yet to report, but he was confident that all of MDSO's operatives had been successfully intercepted and the auction could proceed smoothly.

The party started to trickle in. One by one, they gathered in the room, pretending to gasp in amazement at the resplendence and the beauty of the garden room and the grandiose upholstery. They made sure to walk around in pairs or as families so as not to arouse any suspicion. Under their breath, they were to mutter their bids as each piece was auctioned off. Of course, the syndicates wanted to corner all the pieces for themselves as they would then control the black market pricing on the set of crown jewels, but John was determined that all the jewels should not go to a single syndicate.

They would bid by pointing at the particular piece of furniture. *The VR map of the room that was visible on their glasses would display what each piece of furniture represented in terms of dollars,* John thought, amused. This would be a mad rush of numbers and some very expensive calculation mistakes, he hoped. Everyone knew this and hated it, but they had to play by his rules, of course.

Starting one, their screens flashed, and there was slow, deliberate pointing to pieces of furniture. The North syndicate was the first off the blocks, of course, and raised a high heavens bid. The other international syndicates beat them with their offers. As the next round of bidding started, John thought to himself, satisfied, *this has gotten off to a really good start.*

"Urgent, the vitalcomm beeped into John's ear. He could not believe it. Somebody had the audacity to disturb his performance in this little game that he so enjoyed!

"What?" he said gruffly.

"Storm here, and the subterfuge worked but partially. The girls are in the tower."

"I know because I can track one of them," Storm said.

John said "This is the one occurrence I will pardon, but nobody, no matter what is going to disturb me during this ceremony. And Storm, take care of it. Agent X should be with you shortly.

"Girls, ok we need to have a plan, the tower is big, and where should we look for him," Melanie said in hushed tones in the mortar room.

"Um, I don't know; since the Aite protocol was activated here, all digital traces will not be a possibility, but that also means that operatives and local law enforcement have been alerted." Tani surmised.

"OK what I can't get my head over is that there is something here or something happening here that Miss Daisy and Miss Sam wanted to check out," Esme said. "What was it?"

It had to be big enough, Melanie thought. "I think he is here today."

"Who? John Adea?" Aurora asked.

"Yes," and since we are the only ones who have seen him, it falls to us to lead law enforcement to him or trap him," Melanie said.

"You are correct," Tani said. "I, too, have been thinking about it. That is why Miss Daisy and Miss Sam did not want us here. In case the mission was compromised, they probably felt we would be the most in danger since we had actually seen him."

"OK, now how do we go about finding him?" Esme asked.

"So he is very proud of his planning and schemes and his intellectual ability," Hailey said thoughtfully, "Is there a way we can use that against him?"

"Yeah, he likes leaving little clues doesn't he, as if it's almost a game for him?" Aurora said.

"What did it say on the card that he left us? Let's start there," Melanie said.

Aurora pulled out her pamphlet., "I took a picture, of course."

Aurora sighed, "The garden room, the mortar room, the ravens, and his phone number."

"Ok, that narrows it down quite a bit. Let's call that number?" Mel said.

Esme dialed the number from her pamphlet.

"Sorry, you have reached a number that is no longer in service..."

Esme said, "No luck, guys, not in service."

"There has to be something there; he is too proud to lead us down a dead-end," Tani said.

Esme dialed again, "Sorry you have reached a number that is no longer in service..." Exasperated, she was about to end the call when Mel said, "Wait, don't hang up."

Sure enough, after about 5 seconds of beeps, an automated voice came over the line: "We are waiting to redirect your call. What is your favorite drink? respond in 10 seconds or the call will end automatically."

The girls frantically thought about answers and said strawberry lemonade. Of course, the call ended. This was meant to be a puzzle of sorts.

Melanie racked her head. She thought back to their conversation with John Adea on the plane.

A minute or so later, with her brows furrowed, Melanie said, "Esme, dial again."

When the audio prompt came, Melanie said, "Gin and tonic." Silence again.

But the call did not hang.

"The county fair and the exquisite plant exhibit are in the garden room."

"Click" the call ended.

"Let's go, girls," Mel said. "Aurora found a way to inform law enforcement and the MDSO operatives."

"Sure thing, Mel," Aurora said.

"We need to leave a trail behind as well, in case they need to follow us. A coat in each room," Mel said.

She dropped her coat in the mortar room as the girls ran toward the garden room.

EIGHTEEN

SHOWDOWN AND RESCUE

John Adea was perturbed. He did not expect this level of tenacity from the younger ones. But if they were anything like Agent Storm, he thought he should have expected this. This was indeed a grave miscalculation on his part. He activated vitalcomm and said "Storm, where are they precisely?"

"In the mortar room, and it looks like they got the auction number." Good investigative abilities. They were not to be underestimated by any means.

"OK, keep an eye out and let me know if any proximity warnings are breached."

Meanwhile, the auction was going well. The jewels had almost been auctioned off completely, and only a few remained; the transactions had been recorded in cryptocurrencies. All that remained was to hand the actual jewels over, and John had a plan for that.

He auctioned off the remaining jewels quickly and asked Evil HQ to activate the jewel map and puzzle code for the winning bidders.

The syndicate representatives loitered around the garden room and were surprised to see some girls walk in unnoticed.

They immediately switched off the VR display and pretended to be admiring the room.

Right behind them was another group of school students chatting excitedly.

The janitor watched carefully as the girls went around the room, and the second group loitered to a corner.

"There is no time," he muttered over vitalcomm. "Storm, why wasn't I warned."

"The tracker did not work; it's still showing the location as the mortar room, but I am in the vicinity, ready and prepared."

"That is not acceptable. I will deal with this incompetence later." John said.

"Oh, hello, young lady. Would you mind stepping over to that group with the other young ladies while I clean this part out?" the janitor said.

"Sure thing, Donnie, let's go."

"Oh My God, is that you again, Mel? And Hailey and Esme? Wait a minute, is this like a mi..." Crystal dropped her voice.

"This is so incredible, guys; I'm so excited to see you!"

"Mel did not say that she ran into you," Hailey said, rather shocked.

"There was no time, Hailey," Mel said.

"Where's the nice coat you were wearing, Mel?" Crystal asked. "You looked so nice in it, gum?"

The girls looked around as they chewed gum and chatted with Crystal and her friend Donnie.

"Thank you," the janitor said as he walked through the door into an adjoining room.

The syndicate members were getting a little restless since this interruption was completely unplanned, and John Adea's auctions were never interrupted. Their VR sets started to blink red almost immediately. As the girls noticed the sets all blinking red at the same time, they knew that something was going down. They instinctively formed a circle. Crystal and Donnie stood on the side, looking shocked. The syndicate members got very nervous and started to advance menacingly toward the girls.

"Hands up," was the last thing the girls heard as they collapsed onto the floor.

NINETEEN

An International Haul

"Oooh, my head hurts, where am I?" Esme asked.

"Don't worry, we are fine," Mel said. "Aurie came through just in the nick of time."

"Mom and Miss Daisy?" Hailey asked.

"They are fine, too." Mr Jones tracked the ambulance using the beacon that was activated as a part of the Aite protocol, and local law enforcement was able to pinpoint the exact location of the vehicle. They found Miss Daisy and Miss Sam bound and unconscious. They looked like they had been the subject of some interrogation, and they found John Adea's card at the location. The same one that he had dropped for us as a clue," Aurora said.

"So, was he caught?" Mel asked.

"No, he was not there," Aurora said.

"Who were the people in the room, and why were they trying to attack us?"

"Turns out this was a major haul of international crime syndicate members," Scotland Yard is very happy and is currently debriefing them at HQ; MDSO will follow soon after," Aurora said.

"The jewels?" Tani asked.

They did an imaging of the garden room, and there are two articles, a chest and a flower vase that had been moved ever so slightly," Aurora said. "And the chest has a code; if they try to force it open, it will explode since it is rigged."

"It's at HQ right now," Aurora said.

"And Cyrstal?" Melanie asked quietly.

"She is nowhere to be seen, Mel," Aurora said. "And before you jump to any conclusions, her parents actually confirmed her school exchange trip. So, whatever she was up to, they didn't know about it. "

"We will analyze these co-incidental run-ins with her later." "Right now, let's put our minds to cracking the code and checking what's inside the chest," Esme said.

John Adea breathed a sigh of relief. The two-and-a-half hour-long crawl through the secret tunnels had drained his energy, but as soon as he was airborne, he had time to reflect. Well, they had gotten one over him this time, but he was pretty sure he would be safe and pondering his next move by the time they got any wiser. Until the next time, he was sure he would run into them again.

"Storm, you redeemed yourself with the clever diversion. Now make sure your cover remains intact, and Agents IX and X will be in touch about your next mission. Your training will resume at HQ." John said as he took to the skies.

TWENTY

AT THE PALACE

The aide met them over tea in Buckingham palace. The girls made their curtseys and snaked on tea and the scrumptious sandwiches. They had met the royal family, gotten their photographs and were now being given the exclusive tour of the palace.

"So, how did you figure out the code." the aide asked.

"Oh, it was the team, of course. John Adea's pride and a little bit of thinking. The phone number that he had on the card was 66663332211- if you summed all the like digits together and then divided by 26, the remainder was the letter code. So XIDB. and it went open sesame," the girls giggled.

"We must compliment you on your courage and your tenacity and wisdom in the face of adversity. The royal family extends its gratitude and watches with interest the exploits of the younger generation of MDSO as they take on the world's cleverest criminals." the elegantly monogrammed note read.

"What was the little note at the bottom of the flower vase?" the aide asked.

"That is what we have to figure out. It was rather cryptic. It said: "We know more than you know. It's the nature of evil. Au revoir," Melanie said.

"I hope your friend is OK," the aide said.

"She is going to be fine. She was rather shocked and alarmed at seeing us faint and then law enforcement rushing in with Aurie. She is back home now," Melanie said.

"Well, we must be going. Thanks for the lovely tour and for the snacks," Aurie said.

"Most certainly, we will be watching your adventures with great enthusiasm."

Back at the hotel, Melanie gathered the girls in the room and, over commspeak, said, "There has been an interesting development. Crystal wants to join the training again, and she will work her way back up to the field."

Hm … another day, another development, another adventure.